# HEIR OF THE HAMPTONS

## A FAKE MARRIAGE ROMANCE

### ERIKA RHYS

*For Christina Ross. Thank you for being a fabulous, generous, hilarious friend, and for having my back throughout the process of writing this book.*

Copyright and Legal Notice:

This publication is protected under the US Copyright Act of 1976 and all other applicable international, federal, state and local laws, and all rights are reserved, including resale rights.

Any trademarks, service marks, product names or named features are assumed to be the property of their respective owners, and are used only for reference. There is no implied endorsement if we use one of these terms. No part of this book may be reproduced in any form by any electronic or mechanical means (including photocopying, recording, or information storage and retrieval) without permission in writing from the author.

First ebook edition © 2017.

Disclaimer:

This is a work of fiction. Any similarity to persons living or dead (unless explicitly noted) is merely coincidental. Copyright © 2017 Erika Rhys. All rights reserved worldwide.

## ALSO BY ERIKA RHYS

Heir of the Hamptons

The Gentlemen's Club, vol. 1

The Gentlemen's Club, vol. 2

The Gentlemen's Club, vol. 3

Over the Edge, vol. 1

Over the Edge, vol. 2

On the Brink, vol. 1

On the Brink, vol. 2

On the Brink, vol. 3

# 1

## RONAN

### New York City

"Why don't you just get married?" my sister Cara said.

"You can't be serious." I picked up my water glass and downed half of it, hoping that its icy contents would stimulate my brain into sparking a fresh idea. In the aftermath of my latest loan rejection from Bank of America, I needed a new plan to save my company, Kingsley Technologies, and I needed it fast. Either that, or I'd be forced to lay off most of my employees, which was a betrayal I wasn't ready to contemplate.

Not that I expected Cara to solve my problems over lunch at Bar Six, a mellow West Village bistro that I hit up regularly for its savory croque-monsieur sandwiches. I adored my outspoken younger sister, but her art degree and career as an aspiring painter hadn't given her a lick of business sense. Still, she was the only one in my family who was always on my side, which was why I had just told her about my financial dilemma. Cara's unwavering support gave me strength, which was exactly what I needed right now.

Cara flicked a strand of her long, straight blond hair away from her face and fixed me with her bright-blue gaze.

"Your share of Grandfather's trust is around fifty million," she said. "Isn't that enough to solve your problems?"

"It's more than enough," I said. "But there's no way to tap that money until I'm thirty-five."

"Think creatively," she said. "Under the terms of the trust, we get unrestricted access to our money when we turn thirty-five or when our father dies or when we marry—whichever happens first."

"I'm two years away from thirty-five, our father is in perfect health, and marriage is out of the question," I said. "When it comes to monogamy, I'm my father's son. You know that about me."

"You're nothing like our father," she said, dipping her fork into her arugula-and-parmesan salad. "He's a chronic liar and cheater—you're neither."

"I know who I am," I said. "Like our father, I'm not a one-woman man. Unlike him, I don't make promises I can't keep."

"You wouldn't have to," Cara said. "Not if your marriage was purely a business arrangement."

I stared at her. "What?"

She rolled her eyes. "Come on, Ronan. I can't believe you haven't thought of this yourself. You've only dated half the women in New York—there must be one of them who would be willing to take a big fat check to marry you."

"It would never work," I said.

"Why not?"

"Lots of reasons."

"Such as?"

"There's no point in even discussing it," I said.

"Then consider this a theoretical discussion," Cara said. "I'm curious. Why are you so sure my idea couldn't work?"

"Two words," I said. "Job qualifications. No woman in her right mind would sign on to be my fake wife. Any woman crazy enough to take it on would lack the brains to carry off the amount of acting involved."

"I get that your fake wife couldn't be just anyone," Cara said. "She'd have to look convincing to Dad and Veronica. She'd have to be trustworthy and intelligent."

"Convincing our father and stepmother would only be scene one of the farce you're proposing," I said. "This imaginary fake wife would have to live with me for two years, pose as my wife in public, and not fall in love with me."

Cara screwed up her face at me. "Ewww. I can't believe you just said that."

I shrugged. "Women like me—they always have."

It was no less than the truth. The genetic lottery had gifted me a handsome face and a muscular six-foot-two body, which I kept toned with regular workouts. And while no woman had ever tempted me to consider a long-term relationship, I had the short-term thing down. Be a nice guy, make the woman I was with feel beautiful, and attend to her pleasure as much as my own. I didn't do commitments, I didn't make promises, and three nights was my self-imposed limit—although in practice, I rarely took it beyond one. Manhattan was filled with gorgeous single women, which made it the perfect playground for a guy like me.

Cara sighed. "I love you, Ronan—but you're a pig."

I flashed her a grin. "Maybe I am—but at least I know who I am. Not every man is cut out for marriage, and those of us who aren't should be honest about it. That's my philosophy."

"Philosophy won't save your business."

"Neither will a fake wife. Veronica's a bitch, but she's not stupid. She'd spot a fake in a minute, and when she did, she'd convince Dad to block my access to the trust."

"Can he still control your trust?" Cara said. "Even if you get married?"

I leaned back in my chair, looked at my sister, and a wave of affection for her swept through me. While her fake marriage idea was crazy, her desire to help meant everything to me. Life hadn't been easy for Cara, but she had the biggest heart of anyone I knew.

At twenty-seven, my little sister had grown into a beautiful woman with a strong resemblance to our mother, who had died when Cara was born. At least I'd had our mother for the first six years of my life. All Cara got was her name—Caroline—and a photo album.

"Dad's the primary trustee," I said. "If he filed a lawsuit claiming that I'd faked a marriage to gain access to the trust, the money would be frozen until the lawsuit was resolved. And if I'd already put some of the trust money into Kingsley Tech, my company could be dragged into court as well."

"To recoup the money?" Cara asked.

"Exactly."

"I guess that makes sense," she said. "And lawsuits can go on forever."

"Now you're seeing the big picture," I said. "Until we turn thirty-five, our father controls the trust. Neither of us can touch it or borrow against it without his approval, which, thanks to Veronica, we'll never get. Remember when I wanted to borrow against my share of the trust to start Kingsley Tech?"

"How could I forget?" Cara said. "Veronica shut *that* down in a heartbeat."

"She's got Dad under her thumb—in every area but one."

"Don't remind me," Cara said with a shudder. "I'm almost certain he's screwing his new secretary, who's totally younger than I am. If Veronica wasn't such a bitch, I might actually feel bad for her."

"Don't," I said. "She married our father for his money and lifestyle. The estate in the Hamptons. The house in Aspen. The townhouse on Sutton Place."

Cara leveled me with a look. "True—but enough about Veronica. Aside from getting married, do you have any other ideas that could save you from laying off your employees?"

"Not yet," I said. "But I'll think of something. I always do."

# 2

## AVA

**Brooklyn, New York
One week later**

There was no ignoring the ugly reality that stared at me from the Excel spreadsheet on the screen of my laptop. Unless I won the lottery in the next two months, found a business partner, or landed the mother of all clients, I'd have to shut down Oasis Floral Design.

I slumped in my desk chair and looked beyond the laptop into the eight-hundred square foot space that I'd rented just over a year ago, with so much hope and so many dreams. When I'd first set foot in this space, I'd been beside myself with excitement. The brick walls and scarred wood floors had been dusty, the large-paned windows grimy, and the tin ceiling covered with cobwebs, but the potential for beauty was there. And the location—on the ground floor of a brick warehouse in the heart of Brooklyn's artsy Dumbo neighborhood—was ideal for an up-and-coming floral designer like me.

The hard truth was that no matter how much I wanted to be up-and-coming, right now, down-and-almost-out was a more accurate description. As I gazed over the workspace that I would soon be forced to give up, the air-conditioning unit for the floral cooler switched on, emitting a dull hum that echoed my despondent state of mind.

My chest tightened, and a lump rose into my throat. Running my own business had been my dream, ever since I completed my art degree and stumbled into my first floral-design job. Flowers were beautiful, and beyond the pleasure that I took in arranging them, I loved creating work that enhanced meaningful moments in my client's lives.

Just then, the door at the far end of the space opened, and my neighbor Mimi's cheerful face and mop of curly red hair appeared in the doorway.

"Have time for a break?" she asked, holding up a white paper bag. "I've brought coffee and freshly baked cinnamon rolls."

I pulled myself together, closed my laptop, and returned her smile. "Sounds good to me," I said. Mimi owned the custom jewelry business next door to my workspace. When I'd first moved into the building, we'd quickly become friends, and coffee together had become a near- daily ritual.

Mimi crossed the room to my desk, handed me a cup of coffee, and sat down in the red bucket chair that faced my desk, a spot she'd long since claimed as her own. Then she set her own coffee cup on the desk, reached into the cinnamon-scented bag she'd brought with her, and pulled out a roll, before passing the bag to me.

"Nothing on earth is more fabulous than hot, fresh pastry," she said as she tore off a small piece of the roll and slipped it into her mouth. She winked at me. "Except maybe a hot, fresh man."

At forty-seven, Mimi was twenty years older than me, but no one would have guessed her to be a day over thirty-five. Her quirky personality and love of life made her seem ageless, and daily yoga sessions kept her curvaceous body in great shape. While she'd never married, she was a woman who both loved men and attracted them with ease, and her active sex life was one of her favorite topics.

"I'll take the pastry," I said. "Just as good—and far less complicated."

"Sex isn't complicated," Mimi said. "Although relationships can be. Take my relationship with pastry. I adore it. I lust after it. Sometimes I even dream about it. But it goes straight to my hips, which creates no end of complications."

I laughed. "You're not fat."

"I could be," she said. "You should see my siblings. My family's a trifecta of food obsession, cooking talent, and fat genes. Moving beyond that unfortunate legacy, smoking weed may keep me chill, but it also gives me the munchies. And while yoga does well by me, there are limits to its superpowers. At this point, I'm fine with my looks, but when I was a teenager? My greatest dream was to wake up one morning, look in the mirror, and discover that I'd suddenly become tall, dark, and slender—like you. But enough about me and my adolescent fantasy life. How are things going? Landed any new clients?"

"I just signed a contract for another corporate event, but it's not until fall."

She met my gaze. "So it's still about surviving the summer months."

"It is," I said. "I've talked to every floral designer I know about picking up part-time work, but I've got just enough events scheduled to make me unattractive as a hire."

"Too many dates blocked off?" she asked.

"Exactly. In an emergency, they might offer me a day or two of work, but a handful of last-minute gigs won't pay the bills."

Mimi furrowed her brow. "You can't lose this space," she said. "Not after all the work and money you've put into it. It was a hole when you moved in, but you've transformed it into a lovely workspace. You even built a walk-in cooler, which amazes me."

"Most of the renovation was scrubbing and painting," I said. "The shelving and worktables were thrift-store scavenge, and the cooler's just an insulated room with shelves and a cheap AC unit—building that room was way less expensive than buying floral refrigerators. The frustrating thing is that with my fall bookings and the weddings I've got scheduled next spring and summer, Oasis is on the verge of making it—if I can squeak through the summer."

"Did you apply for the small business loan we talked about?" Mimi asked.

"I did, but the bank turned me down because I have no assets."

"And you don't have any family who might help?"

I shook my head. "Not since my grandparents died."

"If you're free the first week of August, I can pay you to work my booth with me at the craft expo," Mimi said. "I know it's not much—"

I reached across the desk and put my hand over hers. "I'd love to work your booth. And your support means the world to me."

She squeezed my hand, before releasing it to reach for her coffee. "That's what friends are for, Ava. I only wish I could do more."

Just then, my iPhone dinged to announce the arrival of a text. I picked up the phone from my desk and glanced at its cracked screen, which in my current financial situation, I couldn't afford to replace.

"It's from Cara," I said, scanning the text. "She wants me to meet her at Blacktail at seven to discuss a potential job."

Mimi's face lit up. "That's fabulous!" she said. "Cara's the young blond woman I met when she came here to see you, right? Isn't she the rich girl you met at Harvard, the one who got you some of your wedding gigs?"

"That's the one," I said. "We were both art majors, which is how we met freshman year. She's my best friend from college—we were roommates from sophomore year through graduation—and she's also the kindest, most generous person on the planet. Most of the wealthy kids at Harvard hung out with each other, but Cara's different. Coming from money eased her path in some ways but not others. Her stepmother hates her, and her father pretty much ignores her."

"Money isn't everything," Mimi said. She glanced at her wristwatch and got to her feet. "But that's a topic for another day. I need to get the hell out of here, because you have only three hours to shut this place down, make yourself gorgeous, and get your ass across the river to Blacktail, where—fingers crossed—a big white wedding job awaits. The kind of wedding that requires masses of flowers."

"May it be so," I said. "May it be so."

# 3

## AVA

When I arrived at Blacktail and noted the chic attire of the clientele who occupied its tables, I was glad that I'd taken the time to apply fresh makeup and change into my favorite little black dress. Located at Pier A, where Battery Park met the Hudson River, the bar's dark, wood-paneled walls, stained-glass ceilings, and retro lighting fixtures gave it a twenties vibe. At seven o'clock, the evening was heading into full swing, and as I glanced around the space in search of Cara, a cheerful din of conversation and clinking glassware filled my ears.

Within seconds, I spotted my friend's sleek blond hair. Seated at a corner table to the left of the bar, she wore a navy-blue sleeveless dress that showed off her flawless figure and toned arms. A full martini waited in front of the chair across from hers, and her own martini glass was half-empty.

"You must have had a rough day," I said when I reached her. "It's not like you to start drinking without me."

She stood to embrace me, but her smile seemed forced. "It's been a hell of a week," she said.

"Tell me about it," I said as we released each other and sat down.

"I will," she said. "But first, I want to hear how things are going with Oasis."

"Nothing's changed since we last spoke," I said and picked up my martini glass. "But you and other friends are doing your best to help me find work, which gives me hope."

"Let's drink to hope," she said and clinked her glass against mine.

As I sipped my martini, I sensed a nervousness in my friend that was unusual for her, but I resisted the urge to push her to confide in me. Although Cara presented a cheerful face to the world, she also had a deeply private side. Something was troubling her, but whatever was on her mind, she'd tell me only when she felt ready to do so.

She put down her glass, looked up, and met my gaze. "The last time we spoke, you said you'd do anything to keep Oasis going. Do you still feel that way?"

"Of course I do," I said. "I'm ready to work my ass off at any job that doesn't conflict with keeping my commitments to my current clients."

"The job I have in mind wouldn't conflict," she said. "But it's not a typical job. It's not what you're expecting."

"I'm open to anything," I said. "Anything. I just want to save my business."

"Before I tell you more, I need you to promise me something."

"What's that?" I asked.

"Whether or not you take this job, you can't say a word about it to anyone."

Bemused, I stared at my friend. She was weirding me out, but I trusted her good intentions.

"I promise," I said. "I won't breathe a word to anyone. Now, can you please just tell me what this mysterious job actually is?"

She leaned forward and lowered her voice. "Marrying my brother."

After several minutes of profound shock, followed by a second round of martinis and an explanation of Cara's brother's financial difficulties, I had the full picture. But while I sympathized with Ronan Kingsley's situation, which had parallels to my own, I couldn't imagine being anyone's fake wife for two years—let alone a society playboy like Cara's brother.

But vodka and the relief of discussing her idea had lifted Cara's spirits, and she was certain that she'd found the perfect solution to everyone's problems.

"My brother's a great guy," she said. "But he's also a man-whore, with horrible taste in women, which is why I have to find the right fake wife for him. With your background, you're perfect."

"What do you mean?" I said. "My background couldn't be more different from yours and Ronan's."

"You went to Harvard."

"On scholarship. As part of the poor-kid quota."

"Doesn't matter," she said. "You might not have grown up with money, but after Harvard, wealth doesn't faze you."

"Actually, it kind of does. I've just learned to conceal my reactions."

"That's all that matters," she said. "You're smart and beautiful. You know how to dress, talk, and blend in. And I'd trust you with my life."

"I've never even met anyone in your family," I said.

"You know I avoid subjecting anyone I care about to Dad and Veronica," she said. "But because of our friendship, you know a lot about them. And also because of our friendship, it's plausible that you and Ronan met through me and fell madly in love."

"On the surface, I suppose it's believable enough," I said. "At least to anyone who believes in happily ever after, which you know I don't —at least not since Brian."

"Your ex-fiancé was a lying, cheating sack of shit."

"He was," I said. "But it's been two years since I dumped Brian, and at this point I'm just grateful that I found out who he was in time to avoid the mistake of marrying him. Some men simply aren't cut out for marriage."

"That's what Ronan says. He says that he could never limit himself to one woman and that he doesn't believe in making promises he can't keep."

"At least Ronan's honest about who he is," I said. "He sounds kind of like Mimi. Her life is a revolving door of men, but she's very upfront that all she wants is a night or two of fun. Meaningless sex isn't my thing, but neither is judging how other people live their lives—as long as they're open about it."

"You and Ronan are both totally trustworthy, which is why this marriage arrangement can work," Cara said. "Everyone benefits, and no one gets hurt. Ronan gets the trust money that belongs to him anyway. His employees get to keep their jobs. As soon as you're legally married and Ronan gets access to his trust, he writes you a check that lets you keep Oasis—and as a side bonus, we get to be sisters for two years."

"In my heart, you're my sister already," I said. "But marrying your brother—even if it would solve a host of problems—just doesn't make sense. It would mean lying to everyone for two years. And you know how I feel about lying."

"You and Ronan wouldn't be lying to everyone," Cara said. "Since the legal part would be real, you'd simply tell people the truth—that the two of you are married." She shrugged. "You know—the Facebook-relationship-status version of your life, which is all most people need to know anyway."

"I get your point, but lying to friends is different."

"How many friends know the full reasons for your breakup with Brian?"

"Just you and Mimi."

"So you'd want to be honest with Mimi," she said. "That could be negotiated."

"What about your friends—and Ronan's?"

"Aside from me, Ronan's only close friend is his business partner, Jack. And apart from Ronan, the only person I really talk to is you."

"What about your family? I know you're not close to any of them except Ronan, but lying to them for two years is still a big deal."

"The rest of my family are chronic liars themselves," Cara said. "Dad lies to Veronica about his constant affairs. Veronica lies to Dad to make my half brother, Aiden, look good or to make me and Ronan look like shit. And Aiden goes along with every whopper of a lie that spews from his mother's Botoxed face."

There was no arguing with Cara. She'd fully convinced herself that a fake marriage between her brother and me was the best solution to both our financial problems. In her mind, the only obstacle between me, Ronan, and a wedding date was the negotiation of what she clearly considered minor details.

However, Ronan himself was supposed to meet us here later tonight, which would let me shut down this crazy idea once and for all. When Cara had told me that she'd arranged for him to meet us, I'd only agreed to stay for two reasons—out of respect for our friendship and because after years of listening to her talk about her older brother, an opportunity to finally meet him was too intriguing to pass up.

"What time is Ronan supposed to arrive?" I asked.

"At eight." Cara checked her wristwatch and then smiled at me. "He'll be here in fifteen minutes."

# 4

## AVA

At eight o'clock sharp, Ronan Kingsley arrived at our table. While I knew him to be a handsome man from photos that Cara had shown me, he was even better looking in person. With dark, cropped hair, designer stubble, and a perfectly fitted dark-gray suit that only enhanced his tall, muscular body, Cara's brother might have stepped off the cover of GQ.

He sat down beside Cara and kissed her cheek, before giving me a winning smile and extending his hand across the table.

"I'm Ronan," he said. "And you must be Ava. I've heard a lot about you."

"Likewise," I said as I reached forward and took his hand. Intense blue eyes met my gaze, and a spark of unexpected attraction jolted through me. Unsettled by my reaction, I withdrew my hand as quickly as I could without seeming rude.

It was then, for the second time that evening, that Cara surprised me.

"I've said everything I have to say," she said. "And I'll have your backs if you decide to go forward with the marriage idea. But the only way this can work is if you two get to know each other." She slung her purse over her shoulder, rose to her feet, and looked at us. "Which is why I'm leaving now. Talk to each other, order some food, and spend an hour or two together. That's all I ask."

"No promises," Ronan said calmly. "But I've wanted to meet Ava for a long time, and tonight's the perfect opportunity." He looked at me. "Ava, would you have dinner with me?"

Something in his deep voice and relaxed demeanor settled my nerves. While his raw male magnetism had caught me off guard, it wasn't surprising that I'd needed a moment to adjust to finding myself this close to such an attractive man. After all, I'd been a virtual hermit for the past two years. After breaking off my engagement to Brian, I hadn't felt like socializing, and by the time I'd recovered from the hurt and anger of my ex-fiancé's betrayal, I'd been working around the clock to get Oasis off the ground.

"Of course," I said. "I'd be more than happy to have dinner with you."

Cara gave us both a huge smile. "Good. I'll catch up with you both tomorrow."

And with that, she turned and walked away. For a long moment, neither Ronan nor I spoke, and as the silence built between us, I struggled to think of what to say. I needed to tell him that while I sympathized with his financial difficulties, I wasn't about to marry him—but where to begin?

"This is weird," Ronan said.

"Kind of surreal," I agreed.

"Let's get one thing straight," he said. "I came here to appease my sister, but while I'm sure you're a great person, I'm not a fan of Cara's fake-marriage idea."

"I feel the same way," I said. "I'd do almost anything to save my business, but the idea of getting married is just over the top."

"Excellent," he said. "Now that we've put that subject to rest, how about some food?"

"Sounds great to me," I said. "I usually eat a bit earlier, so I'm kind of ravenous."

He signaled a nearby waiter, who hurried over, took Ronan's request for a glass of Scotch and mine for a bottle of mineral water, and handed us each a menu.

"Want to share a side order of fries?" Ronan asked.

"Absolutely," I said. "Who doesn't love fries? For my entrée, I'm going with the sirloin."

"Good choice," he said, flashing me a grin. "I'm planning to have the same."

I closed my menu and smiled back at him. Now that we'd cleared the air, I felt free to sit back and enjoy what promised to be a delicious meal, with no other expectations on either side.

After our waiter brought Ronan his Scotch and took our order, we settled into an easy conversation, which continued throughout the meal. Over dinner, we swapped stories about our lives and work, and Ronan made me laugh with a few humorous anecdotes about himself and Cara. Over dessert, we discovered a common interest in classic American cinema and sparred over whether *Rear Window* or *North by Northwest* was Hitchcock's best movie. By the time we parted ways just outside the Bowling Green subway station, where Ronan had insisted on walking me, it was nearly eleven o'clock.

"Thank you for having dinner with me," he said. "I'm glad that we finally got to meet, although I would have preferred that our first meeting happen under different circumstances."

"The pleasure was all mine," I said. "Since starting Oasis, I don't get out much, and when I do, it's rare to run into a fellow Hitchcock fan."

His face split in a broad smile. "If I was in the market for a wife, she'd have to be a Hitchcock fan."

I laughed and gave him a thumbs-up. "Good taste in movies is on my top-ten list too."

"Now that we've met, I'm sure that we'll run into each other again," he said.

"I'm sure that we will," I said. "Good night—and best of luck with your business."

"Thank you," he said. "I wish you the same."

And with that, he turned and walked away. As I descended the stairs to the subway platform, a glow of satisfaction filled me. Although the evening hadn't ended the way I'd hoped—with a new wedding client for Oasis—it had brightened my spirits. Cara's desire to help meant the world to me, and as it turned out, I hadn't had to disappoint Ronan, either. His reaction to Cara's crazy marriage idea had been similar to my own.

With an ear-splitting screech, the train from Manhattan to Brooklyn braked to a halt in front of me, and as I stepped aboard and took a seat, my sense of well-being stayed with me. While my financial situation was on the verge of becoming dire, I could scrape by for another month or two. Tomorrow morning, instead of staring at depressing spreadsheets and sinking into despair, I would focus on generating creative ideas and finding work.

And somehow, I would find a way to save my business.

# 5

## RONAN

"Where's your head today?" my business partner Jack said to me from his seat on the opposite side of my desk. "I need you to focus on this contract, which has to go out within hours."

"Sorry," I said. "Too many thoughts buzzing around in my head to focus."

"Talk to me," Jack said. "Tell me what's on your mind."

I stood up from my desk, walked to the glass wall of my spacious corner office, and gazed over the rooftops of Manhattan. While I owned the majority of Kingsley Technologies, Jack was a significant shareholder as well. We'd been best buddies since rowing crew together in college, and from the day that he'd joined me at Kingsley Tech, two years after I started it, we'd run the company together. Over the years since, he'd become my closest friend. Like me, he was a confirmed bachelor with good looks, a full head of hair, and the kind of build that got women's attention. We often began evenings barhopping together, splitting off when either of us spotted a woman we wanted to pursue.

"Remember my sister Cara's wacky idea?" I said.

"How could I forget?" Jack said with a chuckle. "Your sister adores you, and she'd cut off her right arm for you—but Ronan Kingsley married? I've got a pretty good imagination, but it doesn't go that far."

I turned to face him. "Last night Cara dragged me to Blacktail to meet the wife she's picked out for me—her best friend from college, Ava Walker."

"That sounds awkward."

"It was—for the first few minutes. But then Cara left us, and I told Ava I wasn't seriously considering the marriage idea; she said that she felt the same way, and we ended up chatting about movies over steak and fries. She was good company, and I enjoyed having dinner with her."

"Sounds like you dodged a bullet," Jack said.

"That's what I thought too," I said as I sat back down at my desk. "But afterward, on the taxi ride home, I started wondering if Cara's idea could actually work."

Jack gave me a knowing look. "This Ava chick must be seriously hot."

"It's not that," I said. "I mean, she's a beautiful woman, in a young Demi Moore kind of way. Tall, dark, slender, and the same age as my sister. But Ava's looks weren't what struck me about her."

"Understood," Jack said. His green eyes twinkled with amusement. "You like your women blond—and stacked. But if it wasn't her looks that grabbed you, what was it?"

"I don't know how to explain it," I said. "She was just so normal. Talking to her was easy—she's smart, and she has a good sense of humor. And she's a class act—articulate, knows how to dress, and a Harvard graduate."

Jack laughed. "Ava sounds like the kind of girl your father and stepmother would pick out for you."

"They'd prefer an heiress, but in every other respect, Ava fits the bill. And a spoiled society princess is out of the question. Way too high maintenance."

"But you think Ava could pass Veronica's inspection?"

"That's the genius of it," I said. "I think she could. If we agreed to live separate lives and file for divorce when I turn thirty-five, getting married could actually work."

"Time out," Jack said. "If you're serious about this, we need to talk pros and cons. There's one huge pro—fifty million bucks—and a hell of a lot of cons. You and Ava would have to fool Veronica, which means that the marriage would have to look real. Ava would need to move in with you. You'd have to live with her for two years."

"My condo's big enough to give us both plenty of privacy," I said. "And I don't think Ava would be a difficult roommate."

"That's a plus," Jack said. "What about your sex life?"

"I always use hotel rooms, anyway."

"What about her sex life?"

"That's a good point," I said. "We'd both have to agree not to bring anyone home."

"I assume she's not seeing anyone serious at the moment," Jack said. "But we're talking two years. What if she meets someone?"

"According to Cara, Ava's not looking for a relationship. She broke off an engagement with some douche named Brian two years ago, and since then, she's been focused on her work."

"What would be her motivation to marry you?"

"A check big enough to save her floral-design business from going under," I said. "The business is based in Dumbo, and it's just her. She didn't strike me as the greedy type, either. I doubt she'd ask for more than a hundred grand or so, but I'd offer her a million."

"That's generous," Jack said.

"I'd be asking for two years of her life. If she carries off a fake marriage for that long, she's earned it."

Jack's expression turned serious. "I don't want to push you into anything—but I hate the thought of laying off half our workforce. We've spent years recruiting the best people, and losing them can't help but set us back."

"So you think I should do it?"

"It's your decision—and I'll support whatever decision you make. But if you marry Ava and tap your trust fund within the next sixty days, that would give us the cash to get the company through this rough patch—and the business would be able to pay you back when the Asian contracts start paying off next year."

"I need to think about it more," I said. "But if I decide to go forward with marrying Ava, I'll need your help with drafting an agreement for us both to sign."

"You'll also need to talk Ava into it," Jack said. "Didn't you say that she thought it was a crazy idea, too?"

"She did," I said. "It's more than likely that she'll turn me down, at least initially. But I can't see any other way of putting my hands on the amount of money we need. And Ava's reliable—Cara's known her for ten years. If I convince Ava to marry me, and we sign an agreement, she'll uphold her end of the bargain."

Jack rose from his chair. "When you come to a decision, let me know." He pointed at the contract sprawled across my desk. "And get that back to me no later than two o'clock with whatever changes you want. OK?"

"No problem," I said as Jack headed toward the door of my office. "I'll get it done."

After he left, I resumed my work on the contract, but as I marked the pages with edits and corrections, a single thought kept circling through my mind.

How could I convince Ava to marry me?

## 6

### AVA

Two days after my bizarre evening with Cara and her brother, I sat at my desk at Oasis, scanning job descriptions on FlexJobs.com. My latest idea was that given my existing commitments, maybe I'd have better luck applying for short-term or flexible positions.

I was scrolling through a job description for a part-time photo editor, wondering if my Photoshop skills were decent enough to apply, when my mail application dinged, and a notification popped up on my screen, announcing the arrival of an e-mail from my accountant. With a sigh, I minimized my browser and opened my e-mail. Not that receiving my tax bill was a surprise—I'd been expecting it for the past week. But given my financial circumstances, knowing what was coming couldn't make writing that check to the IRS any less painful.

Then I saw the number, and my blood froze. Eight thousand dollars? How was that even possible? My accountant, a mild-mannered, middle-aged man named Barry, had led me to expect a bill for less than half that amount. For a long moment, I just stared at the number on my screen, and as I did, my anger grew. Either Barry had fucked up the estimate, or he'd fucked up my tax return. This was outrageous, and after the week I'd had, I wasn't about to let his incompetent ass off the hook.

I grabbed my phone and dialed Barry's number.

"I need to speak with Barry," I said when his receptionist answered. "No, it's not a question you can answer. Tell Barry it's Ava Walker from Oasis Floral, and get him on the line."

When he picked up, I lit into him. "What the hell, Barry? This tax bill is more than twice your estimate!"

He floundered through a half-assed explanation that only added fuel to my rage, and when he started blathering about deductions and amortization, my last shred of patience went up in smoke.

"Cut the bullshit, Barry. It only makes you look even more unprofessional than you already are! The truth is that you screwed up somewhere, and because the return has to be filed by the end of the week, I don't have time to figure it out. File a six-month extension, and file it today. I'll expect an e-mail copy tomorrow."

And with that, I ended the call.

Adrenaline racing through my veins, I jumped to my feet and paced back and forth in front of my desk. Barry's initial estimate had seemed low, but I was no tax expert, and truth be told, I'd wanted to believe it. Filing the extension would put off the tax bill for six months, but in October, I'd have to write the IRS a check for $8,000 —$5,000 more than Barry's initial estimate.

How could I possibly save Oasis, when everything was stacked against me? Not for the first time, the irony of my business name struck me. When I'd come up with the name, I'd envisioned my little business as a flower-filled haven of creativity and fulfilling work, but what had it become? A financial quagmire that grew deeper with every passing day.

Tears of frustration crept into my eyes, and I brushed them away angrily. Getting emotional wouldn't save my business. The only thing that would was a way to make serious money, and if I didn't find it soon, my dream of running my own business would die—together with the piece of my heart that had gone into it.

Just then, a knock sounded against the door.

"Come in," I called as I hurried to the door. While the knocker was likely building management or one of my neighbors, it could also be a prospective client. Since my business focused on events, I didn't get many walk-ins, especially this late in the day, but it was always a possibility.

The door opened, and Ronan Kingsley stepped inside. As on the evening I'd met him, he wore a beautifully tailored dark suit, and he carried an expensive-looking leather briefcase in one hand. Despite the emotion that still simmered inside me from the bad news I had just received, I couldn't help but be struck by how handsome he was. His broad shoulders and powerful chest tapered to a trim waist, combined with his height and dark good looks to give him a commanding presence. As he glanced around the room, taking in my renovated space and repainted thrift-store furniture, I realized how dingy and shabby it must look to him.

"Hi, Ava," he said. "Can I have a few minutes of your time?"

"Of course," I said. I gestured toward the red bucket chair in front of my desk. "Let's sit down."

As we walked toward my desk, questions flooded my mind. Why was he here? It couldn't be about a floral job—or could it? I usually dealt with event coordinators—not CEOs like Ronan—but maybe the fact that we had met through Cara made him feel that he should speak with me personally. But even then, why wouldn't he call, instead of crossing the river from Manhattan to Brooklyn?

When we were seated, I closed my laptop, pushed it aside, and faced Ronan. "How can I help you?"

He cleared his throat and met my gaze. "When we had dinner, you impressed me as someone whom I can trust. With that in mind, I'm here to propose an arrangement."

A suspicion entered my mind, but I dismissed it. When I'd had dinner with him, his rejection of Cara's marriage idea had been very clear—no less so than my own.

"What kind of arrangement are you looking for?" I asked.

"I need a wife within sixty days," he said. "And I want her to be you."

My jaw dropped. Was this some kind of joke? But the expression on Ronan's face was stern and unsmiling. His gaze was direct, and his lips were set in a resolute line.

I looked down for a moment to collect myself, before looking up to face him. "Two days ago, we enjoyed a pleasant dinner together, during which we agreed that Cara's idea is ridiculous. Why on earth would you change your mind? You can't possibly be serious."

"I couldn't be more serious," he said. "You know what's at stake."

He wasn't joking. Ronan Kingsley wanted me to marry him.

"I sympathize with your situation," I said. "You know I do. But I'm no actress, and I'd make a terrible fake wife."

"I disagree," he said. "Cara was right. You're perfect for the job."

The irony of his words didn't escape me. Perfect for the job. Words I'd longed to hear, after the polite rejections that had filled the last few months. Words that would have lifted my mood into the stratosphere—if the job in question hadn't involved a two-year commitment and a marriage license.

"You're talking about two years of our lives, Ronan," I said. "Two years."

He leaned back in his chair and gazed at me. "What are you planning to do with those two years, Ava? Find Mr. Right? Start a family?"

"No—at least not yet. I do want those things someday, but first I want to build my business into something sustainable. I want to support myself doing work that I love."

"Then you should consider my offer," he said. "With what I'm prepared to pay you, you'll not only be able to keep the lights on but also have extra cash to invest in your business. In your future. To sweeten the deal, if you agree to marry me, I'll use my connections to help you. For example, what could a few well-placed magazine articles do for Oasis?"

Stunned into silence, I just stared at him. The visibility from even one magazine article about Oasis could change everything for me—and he knew it.

"Am I getting through to you?" he said.

He was—but I wasn't about to give him the satisfaction of admitting it. After strolling into my office and dropping this mother of a bombshell on me, he didn't deserve to know my every thought.

"I'm more than a little surprised by all this," I said. "I need time to think."

His face relaxed. "I understand. But what you need to understand is that time is running out." He reached into his briefcase, pulled out a thick folder, and placed it on my desk. "Today's a busy day, and I need to run, but the document inside this folder contains the specifics of the arrangement I'm proposing. My contact information is inside, and I've also enclosed a digital copy that you can e-mail to your lawyer. For obvious reasons, aside from talking to your lawyer or my sister, Cara, I need you to keep this discussion and the agreement confidential."

"OK," I said. "I'll consider your offer. I don't have a lawyer, but in lieu of a lawyer, I want to discuss your offer with both Cara and one other close friend, Mimi, who's also completely trustworthy."

"That's reasonable," he said. "The most important thing is that you read the agreement carefully, and consider all its provisions."

I nodded. "I'll do that."

He stood. "I need to get back to my office before five. Let me know when you've arrived at a decision." He turned away and strode toward the exit. When he reached it, he turned back toward me.

"Think quickly, Ava. The offer's good for forty-eight hours."

And with that, he was gone.

# 7

## AVA

After Ronan left, I opened the agreement and began reading. When I reached the section that detailed my compensation, my head spun.

A million dollars?

I stared at the numbers. Fifty thousand on signing. Two hundred thousand on marriage. A quarter million in monthly payments spread over two years. And a lump-sum payment of half a million dollars at the end of the two-year contract.

I shook my head to clear it. In the space of an hour, I'd gone from stressing over an $8,000 tax bill to trying to wrap my head around an opportunity to become a millionaire.

With the initial payment, I could keep Oasis and invest in building and advertising my business. With the second payment, I could consider moving the business to a more high-profile location in Manhattan, a move that would bring me closer to my target clientele. In combination with the media exposure that Ronan had promised, the money he was offering could secure my business—and my future.

There was no doubt about it—a million dollars could change my life. Permanently. If pulling off two years as Ronan's fake wife was even remotely possible, I needed to find a way to make it work.

I flipped the pages of the agreement to the section that listed my obligations and read them over again. While I would need to leave my Bushwick studio apartment and move into Ronan's East Village condo, I would have my own bedroom and bath. I would need to attend an occasional social event as his wife, but the agreement stated that he would be responsible for all related expenses. We would announce our engagement immediately and get married in early May—two months from now. While I would need to play a role in the wedding preparations, after the wedding, most of my time would be my own. Beyond sharing an apartment with him, marrying him, and attending an occasional event on his arm, our lives would remain separate.

Ronan's list of requirements made his intentions clear. He expected no more than the minimum necessary to create the appearance of a real marriage, and he was prepared to compensate me generously for the time and effort involved. But his proposal also left me with a hell of a lot of questions. Could his proposed arrangement actually fool his father and stepmother? What were the risks involved? And what would living with him be like?

I didn't even begin to know how to answer these questions. But Cara would. I picked up the phone to call her and then hesitated. This had been Cara's idea from the beginning, and her enthusiasm for it was clear. Before raising her hopes, I needed to ground myself in the reality of the commitment I was considering.

With that in mind, I got up from my desk and headed next door to talk to Mimi. When I stepped inside her jewelry studio, she was seated on a stool at her workbench, hunched over several small pieces of silver with a soldering iron in her right hand.

"Do you have a minute?" I said. "There's something I'd like to discuss with you."

She rested her soldering iron on its stand, wiped her hands on her leather apron, and shoved a stray tendril of her curly red hair from her face as she turned to me.

"I can spare a few minutes," she said and gestured at a nearby stool. "Have a seat."

I sat down facing her. "I'm not sure where to begin."

Her face brightened. "You've met a man, haven't you?"

"In a way, I guess I have."

She beamed at me. "I'm so happy for you, Ava. You're a gorgeous young woman, you've been alone far too long, and you deserve all the happiness in the world."

"It's not like that," I said. "It's complicated."

"How?" She furrowed her brow. "Don't tell me he's married."

"No—he's single."

"If he's single, then what's the problem?" she said. "Who is he?"

"His name is Ronan."

"Ronan," she said. "I like it. Tell me, is Ronan as sexy as his name?"

"He's very handsome, but—"

"Girl, you haven't gotten any for two years. If he's single and good looking, what's stopping you? I know you're stressed about money, but you only live once. Seriously. Even if you and Ronan aren't destined to get married and live happily ever after, what the hell? Live a little. Have some fun."

"This isn't about fun," I said. "It's about business."

"So that's the complication," she said. "You met Ronan through work, and you're concerned that starting a relationship could make the two of you look unprofessional."

I took a deep breath and then put it out there. "No. Ronan's my friend Cara's older brother. And he's offered me a million bucks to be his fake wife."

# 8

## AVA

After Mimi recovered from her shock at my revelation and read through Ronan's contract, she opened the tin of marijuana that always sat against the back of her workbench, rolled herself a thick joint, and lit up.

"Sure you don't want a toke?" she asked. "I've never seen you this stressed."

I shook my head. "You know I never smoke anything. I tried marijuana once in college, but it did nothing for me."

"You don't know what you're missing," she said, leaning back and exhaling a stream of smoke toward the ceiling. "This is an Alaskan strain called Manatuska Thunderfuck, and it's as mellow as a good lay. Not to mention perfectly legal, thanks to the joys of medical marijuana."

"Thanks, but I'll pass."

She brought the joint to her lips and took another hit. "So this marriage is all about Ronan getting access to his fifty-million-dollar trust fund," she said. "Who are the Kingsleys, anyway?"

"I've never met the rest of the family," I said. "But here's what I know from Cara. Her grandfather founded a Wall Street firm, Kingsley Capital, which is the source of the family fortune. Her father, Carter Kingsley, owns the firm and controls the money. Carter's three children—Ronan, Cara, and Aiden—have equal shares in a trust fund that was set up for them by their grandfather with their father as trustee. They get access to their money when they marry or turn thirty-five—whichever happens first."

"Wait a minute," Mimi said. "I'm no expert on trust funds, but why can't Ronan just borrow against his trust? Why does he have to get married?"

"It's complicated," I said. "Ronan and Cara's mother died when Cara was born. A year or so later, Carter married a Manhattan socialite named Veronica, who's the mother of Aiden, the younger son. Veronica's always hated Ronan and Cara—but especially Ronan. She sees him as competition to her own son. Due to Veronica's manipulation, Carter and Ronan don't get along either, and Carter has long refused to allow Ronan to borrow against his trust for any reason."

"But isn't it Ronan's money?"

"Yes, but until Ronan marries or turns thirty-five, Carter controls the trust, and as trustee, he would have to sign off on any loan against it. Cara suspects that Veronica's ultimate goal is to convince Carter to leave all or most of his fortune to her son, Aiden, and to deny her stepchildren as much of their inheritance as possible."

"Trust funds, inheritances, and an evil stepmother," Mimi said. "How rich *are* these people?"

"Carter Kingsley's on the *Forbes* list," I said.

Mimi's eyes widened. "Cara's father is a billionaire?"

"He is."

"When I met Cara, she didn't strike me as a spoiled rich girl," Mimi said. "You can tell she comes from money, but I never would have guessed that her father's a billionaire."

"Cara would take that as a compliment. She's nothing if not down-to-earth, and she's one of the most unselfish people I've ever known."

"Well, with fifty million coming his way, Ronan can afford to pay you a million bucks to marry him." Mimi stubbed her joint out in the small clay bowl she kept on her workbench for that purpose. "And two years isn't as long as you think. If you can make it work, you should do it."

"I'm tempted. That kind of money would change my life. But I have to consider the long-term implications. If I go through with this fake marriage, at the end of it, I'll be a divorcée, still searching for Mr. Right. And while I'm in no rush, I do want a true marriage and children someday. Will a divorce in my past make men see me as damaged goods?"

"Some will," Mimi said. "But Ronan's contract specifies an amicable, no-fault divorce. Anyone who judges you for that doesn't deserve to be with you—and you sure as hell don't want to be with him."

"I hadn't thought of it that way, but you're right. And marrying Ronan would certainly solve my financial problems."

"It would. I'm glad you're taking this opportunity seriously, because it's tough for creatives like us to make a living. I was pushing forty before my jewelry business became successful enough for me to quit waiting tables at night. Ronan's offer seems solid, and it could secure your financial future."

"I agree. But I have questions about the risks involved, and I only have two days to make a decision. When I contact Ronan, I need to be prepared to request any additions or changes I want to the agreement."

Mimi tipped her head back and looked thoughtful. "Why don't you send Cara a copy of the agreement and set up a working lunch tomorrow with the three of us?"

"That's a great idea," I said. "I can pick up sandwiches and coffee from the deli down the street, and we can eat at one of my worktables."

"Since Cara knows everyone involved, her support will be invaluable," Mimi said. "If the three of us put our heads together, we should be able to figure out any necessary changes to the contract."

∽

The following day, Cara, Mimi, and I sat down around one of my worktables that I had set up with our sandwiches and coffee.

"Have you had a chance to look at the agreement?" I asked Cara. When I'd called her the previous evening, she hadn't picked up, so I'd sent her an e-mail with the contract attached. When she'd e-mailed me back this morning to confirm lunch, she'd written that she'd been at a fundraiser the previous night, which explained why she hadn't answered her phone, but her e-mail hadn't said a word about the contract.

"I read it this morning before I e-mailed you," she said. "And when I did, I saw issues that needed to be discussed face-to-face. There's no point in going forward with the contract as it stands."

"Why not?" Mimi said.

"My brother's delusional," Cara said. "In this contract, it's crystal clear that Ronan expects to continue his current lifestyle."

"The agreement stipulates that neither of us can bring sexual partners back to Ronan's apartment, which seems fair enough," I said. "I don't plan on hooking up, but why should I care if he does?"

Cara looked at me and then at Mimi. "Neither of you have met my stepmother, Veronica," she said. "You don't know what she's capable of."

"Tell us," Mimi said.

"When Ronan announces his intention to marry Ava, Veronica's going to be as suspicious as hell. And she's nothing if not a hub for gossip. Although she spends most of her time at the Southampton estate, she has tons of bitchy friends in Manhattan. If Ronan's out screwing around, Veronica will hear of it."

"From everything you've ever told me about Veronica, I get that she'll be suspicious from day one," I said. "What I don't know is what she'll do about her suspicions."

Cara pursed her lips in thought. "Initially, she'll deploy her usual tactics. She might invite you to lunch or tea and cross-examine you about your relationship with Ronan. Or she might drop in on you and Ronan at his apartment, which needs to look like you share a bed—but that's manageable. I know Ronan's apartment, I know what Veronica will look for, and I've already figured out how to stage everything."

"So lunch, questions, and a drop-in or two," I said. "With your help, I think I can survive that."

"But if Ronan's behavior gives Veronica any reason to believe that your marriage is fake, she'll make it her mission to find proof," Cara said. "I wouldn't put it past my witch of a stepmother to hire private investigators to trail you and Ronan around with cameras. And the minute she gets her hands on evidence suggesting the marriage isn't real, bye-bye trust fund. She'll take her evidence to my father, convince him to sue Ronan, and the day that suit is filed, Ronan will lose access to the trust."

"What does losing access mean?" I asked. "Does Ronan get to keep the money he's already taken out?"

"Not necessarily," Cara said. "My father has a fleet of lawyers at his disposal, and if he turns those sharks loose, all bets are off. Shutting off Ronan's access to the trust would only be the beginning. They could also launch a lawsuit aimed at recouping whatever money Ronan's already taken from the trust."

"What's the point of a lawsuit?" Mimi said. "Won't Ronan get the money when he turns thirty-five, anyway?"

"He will," Cara said. "But between now and then, a lawsuit could land him in even hotter financial water than he's in already. And destroying Ronan's business would be a dream come true for Veronica."

"We can't let that happen," I said. "You've told me how hard Ronan's worked to build Kingsley Tech."

"Could Ava be sued as well?" Mimi asked.

"Ronan would be the primary target," Cara said. "But it's possible that my father's lawyers would sue Ava for the return of any money she receives from Ronan."

"Because that money could be viewed as coming from the trust?" I asked.

"Exactly," Cara said. "That's why if you and Ronan go through with this marriage, you need to commit to it one hundred percent."

"A lawsuit could destroy both Ronan and me," I said. "You're right, Cara. While I have no desire to control Ronan's personal life, it's far too risky for either of us to have affairs."

Mimi sipped her coffee and nodded in agreement. "It's unfortunate that you and Ronan have to limit your freedom," she said. "But with Veronica watching for any opportunity to take you down, there's no way around it. The two of you have to put your sex lives on ice—unless, of course, you decide to have sex with each other."

"Not happening," I said. "Casual hookups aren't my thing. If doing this right means swearing off sex for two years, I can cope. I haven't been with a man since my ex-fiancé, and while I do miss sex, I'm capable of living without it. The question is whether Ronan's willing to do the same."

"It needs to go in the agreement," Cara said. "No hookups whatsoever. On either side. If Ronan refuses to make that commitment, walk away. I want to help my brother, but there's no point in creating a situation that's doomed to blow up in everyone's face."

I made a note on my notepad. "No hookups, then."

"Not strong enough," Mimi said. "This agreement needs to be rock-solid, which means some kind of penalty if either of you break it." She raised an eyebrow at me. "No woman should stake a nickel on a wayward cock—let alone a million bucks."

"That's a great idea," Cara said. "We need to protect Ronan against himself."

"How about if I edit the termination clause?" I said. "It already states that breaking the agreement will result in an immediate parting of ways, followed by a quick, no-fault divorce. I can just add financial penalties for whoever breaks it."

"That should do it," Mimi said.

"There's one more thing that worries me," I said. "So far, I've met Ronan twice, and I feel like I've seen two different men. At Blacktail, he was relaxed and conversational. He was someone who I could live with. Yesterday, when he came here to offer me this agreement, he was another person. Not that he was rude or anything like that—more abrupt and aggressive."

"That's his business persona," Cara said. "As men go, my brother's a nice guy. He's kind and generous. Within the limits of his testosterone-fueled brain, he can even be thoughtful. But he's also a ruthless negotiator, and he likes to win."

"If I go through with this, which Ronan will I be living with?" I asked. "Mr. Nice Guy or Mr. Negotiator?"

"Mr. Nice Guy," Cara said promptly. "With occasional flashes of Mr. Negotiator, if you try to share a television remote or play a video game. Ronan's got a hardcore competitive streak. When he makes up his mind that he wants something, he sets out to get it—and there's no stopping him."

"Fortunately, Ava's no shrinking violet," Mimi said with a chuckle. "If she and Ronan get into a battle for the remote, my money's on Ava."

"I have my own television, which I'll put in my room," I said. "No TV-related conflicts will disturb our marital harmony."

Cara laughed. "Good call. Because when it comes to determination, you and my brother might as well be twins. Just think of this as moving in with the male version of you."

I rolled my eyes. "Except I'm not a whore."

Cara's lips parted in a wide smile. "If Ronan signs the revised agreement, for the next two years, neither is he."

# 9

## RONAN

Several hours before the forty-eight-hour mark, Ava e-mailed me to say that she had considered my offer and that she wanted to discuss a few details before signing it, which she suggested could happen at my office at four o'clock this afternoon.

Relieved, I shot back an e-mail confirming our meeting and then headed for the office next door to tell Jack.

"Good news," I said, after I'd entered Jack's office and shut the door behind me. "I've closed the deal with Ava. She's coming here at four to go over a few details and sign."

"You're the man," Jack said. He leaned back in his desk chair and grinned at me. "How many guys can say they pulled off a forty-eight-hour courtship?"

"I can't take all the credit," I said as I sat down in the chair across from him. "Cara found Ava, and you helped me draft the agreement."

"It was the least I could do," Jack said. "Thanks to you, our problems are solved."

"The next year certainly looks a hell of a lot easier," I agreed. "Over the next two months, the wedding arrangements will eat up some of my time, but I've come up with a plan to minimize that."

"What's your plan?" Jack asked.

"We'll get married at my father's Southampton estate," I said. "That way, Ava and I won't have to waste time searching for a venue. I'll tell Veronica that we're fine with her usual caterers and that she and my father can invite whoever the hell they want. In general, I intend to let Veronica plan this wedding however she likes and advise Ava to do the same."

"Ava's going to want to pick out her own dress," Jack said. "Not to mention bridesmaids and their dresses. Women start planning that shit as soon as they're old enough to flip the pages of *Vogue*."

I shrugged. "Fine by me. Ava's got good taste."

"And if you're letting Veronica handle the guest list, you'll need to make sure that invitations go out to Ava's family or whoever Ava wants to be there," Jack said. "Remember how Veronica 'forgot' to invite me to your college graduation party?"

"Good point," I said. "I have to protect Ava from Veronica in every way I can. But I don't have to worry about Veronica fucking with Ava's family, because she doesn't have any. Cara gave me the rundown when she was pitching Ava to me as my fake wife."

"No family?" Jack said. "What's her story?"

"Her parents died in a plane crash when she was a kid. She was their only child, and her maternal grandparents raised her—but her grandmother died the year she started college, and her grandfather a year or so later."

"Damn," Jack said. "That's tough."

"It is," I agreed. "I may not get along with most of my family, but my relationship with my sister means the world to me."

"Cara's a great girl, and your relationship with Aiden could improve over time," Jack said.

"My half brother's a pussy," I said. "At twenty-five, he's still Veronica's pawn."

"Ugly," Jack said, shaking his head. "But twenty-five is young.

Don't be too hard on your kid brother. There's still time for him to grow a pair."

"I'm not holding my breath," I said as I got to my feet and prepared to leave. "I'll be in my office working on the IBM proposal. I should have time to get through the financials before my meeting with Ava."

"After Ava signs the agreement, let's go out for a drink," Jack said. "We'll raise a glass to Kingsley Tech's future, and check out whatever hot women Manhattan brings our way."

I gave him a thumbs-up. "It's a plan."

# 10

## RONAN

When Ava stepped into my office at four o'clock, she was dressed for business in an elegant pale-gray suit that flattered her slender figure. Her skirt ended just above her knees, and her heels accentuated a pair of nicely toned legs. A black leather tote bag hung from her right shoulder. While I liked my women blond and busty, Ava was more than attractive enough to make any man take a second look.

"Thank you for making the trek across the river," I said.

"Not a big deal," she said. "You made the trip last time, so this time it's my turn."

Was there a hint of nervousness in her voice? I wasn't sure, so I tried to put her at ease. The last thing I wanted was for her to get cold feet now.

"Make yourself comfortable," I said, gesturing at the chair in front of my desk. "Would you like coffee or a glass of water?"

"Thank you, but I'm fine," she said as she sat down across from me. "I'd like to discuss two adjustments to the contract before we sign."

Her willingness to sign came as a relief, and I leaned back in my chair and regarded her.

"What adjustments would you like?"

"A requirement of no extramarital sex for either of us, and financial penalties if either of us breaks the agreement."

Annoyance simmered in my gut, but I kept my voice calm.

"Where's this coming from, Ava? Why should you care whom I fuck?"

"I don't," she said coolly. "This isn't personal."

"In that case, I'm going to repeat my question. Where's this coming from?"

"Before I contacted you to set up this meeting, I talked to Cara," she said. "Your sister made a very convincing case that if either of us fools around—especially you—that Veronica will hear of it through gossip and take steps to confirm her suspicions. I don't want our fake marriage to blow up into a legal nightmare."

I weighed the issue for a moment before coming to a decision. "Cara's correct that we need to be discreet because of Veronica. I'll agree to financial penalties if either of us gets caught hooking up with anyone. But that's as far as I'm willing to go."

She shook her head. "That's not far enough."

My temper flared. "You can't expect me to live like a monk for two years."

"Given what's at stake for both of us, I don't see any other way."

"You're being unreasonable," I said. "Men have needs."

Her eyes flashed. "So do women, but unlike you, I'm prepared to make the necessary sacrifices for this to work."

"You're out of your mind," I said. "I'm a healthy, horny guy. How do you expect me to live without sex for two fucking years?"

She glared at me. "Porn? A blow-up sex doll? Your right fucking hand?"

Ava wasn't seeing our arrangement the way she should have,

which pissed me off. But damn it, the woman knew how to put up a fight.

"Why not simply agree to keep our personal lives discreet?" I said. "I've already agreed to add financial penalties to the contract, which would give us both additional incentive for discretion."

"Too risky," she said dismissively. "Did you listen to a word of your sister's advice? Cara's been more than clear that your stepmother's going to be suspicious no matter what we do, and that she may well hire investigators to follow us. If Veronica scores a photo or two of you with some random chick and uses those photos to sic your father's lawyers on us, it's impossible to predict how far they'll go."

"That won't happen," I said.

"Not if you keep your dick in your pants—but apparently, that's not an option. I'm prepared to give up two years of my life, but I'm not willing to get dragged into a lawsuit."

"It won't happen," I said.

"You can't deny that it could."

"It won't."

Ava stood to her feet. "You're right, Ronan. It won't happen—because I'm done here." She reached into her tote bag, pulled out the folder I'd given her two days before, and tossed it on my desk. "Here are the copies of the agreement that you gave me. I wish you the best of luck in solving your financial problems. But I need to find a different way of solving mine."

And with that, she turned and glided toward the door. My gut clenched as I felt my hopes leaving with her.

"Wait a minute," I called after her.

She stopped and turned toward me. "What the hell for?"

"Give me a minute to think," I said.

Could I sign away my life for two years? If I didn't, then I was back in a quagmire of financial problems, two hours after I'd told Jack that I had everything under control.

I didn't have time to look for another fake wife, and even if I did, it would be next to impossible to find one as ideal as Ava. And if things fell apart with her, I wouldn't be able to rely on my sister's help to find another woman to marry. Cara would blame me for screwing things up with Ava, and she'd be furious with me.

Too much was on the line, and with the clock running out, it was time to man up.

So I steeled myself to make the most unwanted deal of my life.

"Come back and sit down, Ava," I said. "Let's discuss your adjustments to the contract."

"My adjustments are nonnegotiable," she said.

"Do you have a draft of the contract with your changes?"

"I do."

"Show it to me."

She walked back to my desk, reached into her bag, and withdrew a folder, which she handed to me. "I've enclosed two copies, one for each of us. The no-hookups requirement is on page four, and the financial penalties have been added to the termination clause at the end of the agreement."

"Have a seat," I said. "It's going to take me a minute to read this."

Ava perched on the chair across from me, and as I read her edits to the contract, I sensed her annoyance coming off her in waves. When we'd had dinner together, I'd suspected that she might have a feisty side, but I hadn't expected a woman who arranged flowers for a living to negotiate so aggressively. Apparently, I was dealing with a real-life steel magnolia. She could probably manhandle a fistful of roses without feeling the stabs of their thorns.

Her no-hookups requirement was straightforward, but when I read her revisions to the termination clause, it floored me. In addition to assigning hefty financial penalties to either of us if we broke the agreement, she'd added a paragraph requiring me to make her whole in the event of any lawsuits arising from my breaking it. I'd not only have to repay any portion of her money that was taken from her but also pay her legal bills and compensate her for any time lost from work.

The little witch had thought of everything, and I looked up at her with new respect.

"The paragraph addressing potential lawsuits is unnecessary," I said. "I'm a man of my word, and if I commit to denying the women of Manhattan for the next two years, you can trust me to do just that."

"Bullshit," she said. "Your history indicates otherwise."

"I've never broken a promise in my life," I said.

She lifted a delicate eyebrow at me. "Maybe not—but you've never promised to keep your pants on, have you?"

Once again, she'd scored, and since I'd already committed to signing my life away, I resigned myself to the inevitable.

"Very well," I said. "I'll agree to leave it in, because it's a moot point anyway. I'll keep my word, and there won't be any lawsuits."

"I hope not," she said. "But if your cock drags both of us into court, you're the one who's going to pay the bill."

Thanks to her, my cock was about to go on lockdown for two years, which was unimaginable to me. But I needed to save Kingsley Tech, and if that meant reviving my relationship with my right hand, then that was what I had to do.

I picked up a pen and signed both copies of the revised contract, before handing the pen and the contracts to her. "Ready to sign?"

For a long moment, she just looked at me.

"What is it now?" I said. "Having second thoughts about signing *your* revised contract?"

Her eyes narrowed. "Not at all," she said, before she leaned forward, signed both copies, and slid one across the desk to me, before dropping the other into her bag.

Relieved that the deal was done, I leaned back in my chair. "So," I said, "we have an agreement, which requires you to move into my apartment within one week. As soon as you've moved in, I'll announce our engagement to my father and stepmother."

She fixed me with a look. "Before I move anything, you've got one more piece of paper to sign," she said. "My fifty-thousand-dollar check. And one more thing, Ronan."

"What's that?"

"Don't cheap out on the ring."

# 11

### AVA

### One week later

"This should do it," Cara said with an air of satisfaction as she adjusted the position of a lamp on an end table. "We've transformed Ronan's boring guest bedroom into an attractive chill space where you can kick your heels off, and while the bath isn't as nice as the one in the master, it's adequate."

"It's nicer than any place I've lived," I said as I stepped back and took in the changes that we had made over the past few days. At Cara's urging, I'd chosen a muted mossy green for the walls, and we'd hung several of her brightly colored abstract paintings. We'd replaced the original bedroom set with a beige leather Chesterfield daybed flanked by antique-white end tables, whose finishes were almost a perfect match to the one piece of furniture I'd kept from my apartment—my grandmother's rolltop desk. Aside from the desk, my television, and a few favorite books, just about everything else had gone to Goodwill, since none of it was worth what it would cost to store it for two years.

"Your concept was spot-on," I said. "Despite looking like a couch, the daybed is super-comfortable, and with the daybed and matching ottoman facing the television, the room gives the impression of being a space for me to retreat to when Ronan takes over the living room to watch football."

"Or shoot zombies with the volume dialed up to eleven," Cara said. "He claims that playing video games relaxes him, which is a mystery to me. What could possibly be relaxing about shooting three monsters while running from six more?"

"I kind of get it," I said. "Video games aren't my thing, but they're one way of releasing stress."

"I suppose," Cara said. "Now that we're done in here, let's review our staging of the rest of the apartment before I head home for the night. We need to make sure that we haven't forgotten anything."

I trailed her down the hall that led to the main living space of Ronan's loft apartment. As we passed the door to his workout room, which was closed, the whirring rhythm that came through the door told me that he was exercising on his rowing machine.

"The vases of fresh flowers were a stroke of genius," Cara said as we entered the living area. "They add a splash of color and signal that there's a woman living here."

"I wanted to contribute something," I said. "The bill for this fake marriage only continues to grow, and Ronan still has to put a rock on my finger."

"A big rock," Cara said. "There's no doing this halfway."

"I told Ronan as much when we signed the paperwork," I said.

She laughed. "You didn't!"

"I did. Given Ronan's financial issues, I want to keep our wedding as inexpensive as possible, but that diamond is an investment in convincing Veronica that Ronan's in love with me. He can sell the ring and get his money back when I return it to him in two years."

"Going too minimal isn't wise," Cara said. "Given that we're talking about a fake marriage, there's no better cover than a big white wedding."

"You've already promised to be my maid of honor, and I imagine Ronan will ask Jack to be his best man," I said. "There's no need for a retinue of bridesmaids and groomsmen."

"It's fine to keep the ceremony brief and simple," Cara said. "Everyone hates long ceremonies, anyway. But the reception and dinner need to be epic. If you and Ronan throw the kind of party that impresses Veronica's society friends, that could go a long way toward convincing her that your marriage is real. If you can use the wedding to push her to that conclusion, the next two years will be a hell of a lot easier for you and Ronan."

"Then I'll do my best to get her there," I said. "If there's anything I know, it's how to throw a good party. Between my floral-design career and the catering jobs I worked during college, I've been part of hundreds of weddings."

"You have," she said. "Which is why I know you've got this."

"At least the wedding part of it," I said. "Thanks to ten years of sweating over wilting flowers, carting trays of lukewarm food, and witnessing bridezilla moments."

"You'd better plan on dishing up a few of those yourself," Cara said. "You don't have to go total bridezilla, but you do have to put your stamp on this wedding—especially since weddings are part of your work. If you don't, my stepmother's suspicions will go through the roof."

"You're right," I said. "I'll find a way to put my stamp on the wedding. Although I'm sure it won't be easy."

"Don't overthink it," Cara said. "Take one step at a time, stay focused on the goal, and remember that I've got your back."

"Thank goodness for that," I said as we entered Ronan's master suite.

Furnished with a king-sized sleigh bed, matching end tables, and several large abstract paintings that were Cara's work, the master bedroom was at the end of a short hallway that connected to separate areas with twin dressing rooms, closets, and baths. Earlier today, Cara and I had purchased duplicates of many of my toiletries and makeup, which we had used to stage the bathroom that was now supposedly mine, and most of my wardrobe now occupied the adjacent dressing room.

Cara stepped into the dressing room, which contained an alcove with a counter, a chair, and a well-lit mirror for applying makeup.

"This room needs a few finishing touches," she said as she glanced around. "We need it to look like you're using it."

I stepped into the bathroom, opened the drawer where I'd stored my makeup, and grabbed two handfuls of items, before returning to the dressing room, where I arranged the items on the counter beneath the mirror.

"How's that?" I asked.

"Good," she said. "But I have another idea that will make it more convincing."

She opened one of the drawers, went through its contents, and pulled out a silk dressing gown and a lacy black brassiere. She draped the dressing gown over the back of the chair and then tossed the brassiere onto its seat.

"There," she said. "Always leave something for the maid to pick up. Staff know everything, and you can't necessarily trust them."

"I didn't realize Ronan had a maid," I said.

"Only a part-time one," Cara said. "Josefina comes in twice a week for a few hours, and the one time I met her, she struck me as a very nice person. It's not that I think she's untrustworthy or anything—I just don't know her well enough to be certain of how she'd respond if Veronica questioned her or offered her a fistful of cash in exchange for information."

"We've mostly talked about your stepmother," I said. "While she's the one most likely to make trouble, what about your father and your half brother, Aiden? What kind of reception should I expect from them?"

"My father's a very busy man," Cara said. "Initially, he'll just accept your engagement at face value. Aiden's a brat, but due to his spoiled existence, he's a young twenty-five and not nearly as savvy as he thinks he is."

"So your father isn't likely to be a problem," I said. "At least not initially. And Aiden doesn't sound too difficult to handle."

"Beyond the occasional snarky comment, he isn't," Cara said. "That said, anything Aiden sees or hears reaches Veronica at the speed of light, so you need to watch your step when he's within earshot." She glanced at her wristwatch. "It's nearly eight, and I need to head home, but call me in the morning. I know you're planning to work at Oasis tomorrow, but we can at least touch base via phone."

"Will do," I said and gave her a big hug. "Thank you for everything."

∽

After Cara left, I returned to the dressing room to grab a few items of clothing that I needed for tonight and tomorrow morning. With Cara gone, and the rush of staging the apartment over, the reality of my commitment sank into me. Although I'd spent most of the past three days in Ronan's apartment, tonight would be the first night that I slept here, and the realization of how much my life was about to change wasn't easy to grasp.

Any more than Ronan was. Over the past three days, he'd mostly ignored Cara and me—until last night. When Cara and I were putting the final touches on the last coat of paint in my bedroom, Ronan appeared with bags of spicy, savory Thai takeout, which the three of us consumed together while engaging in a spirited discussion about the Yankees' odds of winning the World Series this year.

Last night, I'd felt the warmth of his attention and sensed why so many women had fallen at his feet—and into his bed. On top of his good looks, which gave Henry Cavill a run for his money, the man could charm paint off walls. When he'd arrived with the takeout, I'd been exhausted and paint-covered, but within minutes he'd made me laugh and relax.

But this morning, when I'd arrived at the apartment to meet the furniture-delivery men, he'd been gruff to the point of surliness and left the apartment before the delivery was even finished.

The man was an enigma. A living, breathing contradiction. And I had signed up to live with him and play his fake wife for two years.

Just then, he appeared in the entrance to the dressing room. It was the first time I'd seen him shirtless, and the sight shot an unexpected bolt of lust to my groin.

Dressed in navy sweat pants that hung low on his trim waist, the perspiration on his brow and the dampness of his dark hair testified to the strenuousness of his just-finished workout. Heat and a trace of musky male scent reached my nostrils, and my lips parted as I took in the thick, defined muscles of his shoulders and chest, which carried a light sheen of sweat. My gaze dipped lower, following the ripples of his corded abs, tracing the line of hair that led downward, before I caught myself and tore my gaze away from the generously sized package that his sweat pants did little to conceal.

With unsteady hands, I resumed stacking the clothes that I had come here to retrieve, hoping that he hadn't noticed me gaping at him.

"Like what you see?" he said.

Annoyed that he'd caught me, I forced myself to meet his eyes. "Looks like you worked up a sweat."

His expression told me that he hadn't bought my cover-up. "Isn't that the point of working out?"

I wrinkled my nose at him. "You could seriously use a shower."

"That's where I'm headed now," he said. "Before I go, is my apartment pretty enough for you yet? You and my sister have been at it for three days."

My annoyance grew. Cara and I had worked our butts off to stage the apartment, and he hadn't lifted a finger to help. On the contrary, aside from the one night he'd deigned to show up with the takeout, the man had gone about his life as if nothing out of the ordinary was taking place around him.

"Cara and I are finished," I said. "If you're done working off your sexual tension, perhaps you'd care to look at what we've done with the guest bedroom."

He leaned against the doorframe and regarded me. "The one with the bed of nails I bought for you?"

Something snapped inside me. "That's right, Ronan," I said sweetly. "The very one. And thank you for the guillotine you put in the shower. That was thoughtful of you."

A slow smile spread across his face, and he released a chuckle. "You're quick."

"Unfortunately, when it comes to your reputation, I've heard the same about you."

His eyes narrowed and his smile vanished. "Unfortunately for you, Ava, finding out the truth isn't part of our contract."

"If it had been, I wouldn't have signed it."

"Your loss," he said, before turning away and disappearing into his dressing area. A second later, a door slammed shut and the water turned on.

I seized my pile of clothes, left the master suite, returned to my room, and closed the door behind me, before dropping the clothes on the ottoman and slumping onto my daybed, my "bed of nails" as Ronan called it.

Bed of nails indeed. When I'd signed the contract with him, I'd believed that I was signing on to marry a nice guy to whom I was mildly attracted. Nothing special, just the whiff of lust that any red-blooded woman would feel toward such a good-looking man.

The last thing I needed was a case of the hots for my soon-to-be fake husband. Beyond his history as a confirmed man-whore, the two of us simply didn't get along. While Ronan was more than capable of turning on the charm, he could also be abrasive and difficult.

Was what I'd felt in the dressing room no more than the consequence of years of celibacy and a sudden, unexpected confrontation with a hotter-than-hell, half-naked man?

With all my heart, I hoped that it was.

# 12

## RONAN

After stepping into the elevator of the building where I lived, I pressed the button for the twelfth floor and girded myself for the evening to come. It was time to move forward with announcing my engagement to my father, and before I made that phone call, I needed to go over this next step with Ava.

Over the past week, the time I'd spent with her had brought me to a few conclusions. On one level, I'd chosen the perfect fake wife. She was bright; she looked and dressed the part; and for a woman, she wasn't high-maintenance. She and Cara had made a fuss over setting up Ava's room, but they had done the work themselves, without attempting to drag me into it. When they finished, the room did look better, and since Ava's move-in four days ago, she'd spent most of her time at her business or in her room. I wasn't crazy about her habit of positioning vases of flowers around the apartment, but flowers were her thing, and I wasn't about to pick a fight over anything so trivial.

Especially when so many of our interactions hadn't ended well. My first impression of Ava's fiery temperament had proven true—and once her temper was up, the sky was the limit. My lips curved at the memory of how she'd responded when I'd caught her checking out my junk. Men and women checked each other out all the time, and I hadn't read anything more into Ava's look, but I couldn't resist teasing her about it, not after catching her midstare.

It wasn't as if I hadn't looked her over too—of course I had. I was just better at not getting caught. Despite her slender build, Ava had a banging body. If we'd met under different circumstances, I would have seduced her by now, but since we lived in the same apartment, sex would muddy the already murky waters that I had hurled myself into with our fake-marriage arrangement. No matter how blue my balls got over the next two years, sex with my wife-to-be wasn't an option.

As the elevator slowed, I reached into my jacket pocket, touched the box containing the engagement ring that I'd picked up at Harry Winston, and focused on my plan for the evening.

I'd open the discussion by presenting Ava with the ring, which should please her, given her stinging comment about not cheaping out on it when we'd signed our contract. Not that her comment had anything to do with the six figures I'd dropped on her ring—it was an investment in the successful launch of our fake marriage.

After growing up around my stepmother and her circle of Botoxed harpies, I knew damned well that when Veronica and her friends set eyes on that ring, its carat count and designer name would guide their initial impression of Ava. There was no way to protect Ava completely from the gauntlet she was about to run, but I intended to give her as much armor as I could. Tonight, that meant giving her the ring and going over the wedding arrangements I planned to make for us.

When the elevator opened, I stepped out, walked to my door, opened it, and stepped into the darkened foyer. Light glimmered from the living area beyond, and when I reached it, Ava was in the kitchen, getting herself a glass of water. Her green zip-front sweater hugged her curves; dark, fitted yoga pants showed off her long, slender legs; and with her back turned to me, her nicely rounded ass was on full view.

"Hi, Ronan," she said, turning to me. "How was your day?"

"Mostly routine," I said. "Do you have time to talk—maybe over a glass of wine?"

"Sure," she said.

I put down my briefcase and loosened my tie, before crossing the kitchen to the wine rack and pulling out a bottle of Barolo, which I opened, while Ava took out two wineglasses. After I filled the glasses and handed one to her, we headed for the living room, where I sat down in my favorite armchair.

Ava sat on the couch opposite me and tucked her bare feet beneath her thighs. "I imagine we need to talk about announcing our engagement," she said.

"We do," I said, lifting my glass toward her. "But before we go there, cheers."

"Cheers," she said, before taking a sip. "Mmmm...this is nice."

"Barolo's one of my favorite wines," I said. With my free hand, I reached into my jacket pocket, withdrew the ring box, and held it out to her. "I picked up an engagement ring today."

She put down her glass and took the dark-blue box from me. "Harry Winston," she said. "I know I said not to cheap out, but you didn't have to go this far."

"Open the box and have a look," I said.

When she did, her eyes widened. "It's stunning, Ronan. It's the most gorgeous ring I've ever seen! But you should return it. Something half its size would be impressive enough, and it must have been crazy expensive."

I smiled at her. "It was—but it also sends the right message."

"I suppose," she said. "But you can't possibly afford this right now. Not with your financial challenges, not to mention the money you're paying me."

Ava's concern surprised me. She'd been nothing if not hard-nosed about the financial aspects of our arrangement, and I wasn't used to anyone other than Cara or Jack worrying about me. "Don't worry about the money," I said. "Once we're married, and I get access to my trust, I'll have more than I need. Now, try it on."

She shook her head. "I'll wear it when you introduce me to your father and stepmother, of course. But it's too valuable to wear around the house."

I put down my wineglass, leaned forward, and reached for her left hand. Like her, her hands were elegant, with long, slender fingers. For a second I wondered what those hands would feel like wrapped around my cock, until my internal censor kicked in and slapped a big red X on that image.

"It's insured," I said as I took the ring from its box and slid it onto her ring finger. "You need to get used to wearing it."

Ava held up her hand and turned it back and forth for a moment, admiring the glittering stones. Then she picked up her glass and looked at me. "Tell me your plans for announcing our engagement."

"I'll call my father tomorrow," I said. "I'll tell him about our engagement. I'll also tell him that we want to get married at the Southampton estate in early May. Once I drop that bomb, you and I need to be ready to answer questions about our wedding plans."

"The first question everyone will ask is how we met," Ava said. "Fortunately, our backstory doesn't need to deviate all that far from the truth."

"I agree. You're Cara's former college roommate, and she introduced us. We just need to backdate that introduction by a few months."

"It's March now, so why don't we say that we met at Cara's New Year's party?" Ava suggested. "I was at that party, and well over a hundred people must have come and gone over the course of the evening—who's to say you weren't one of them?"

I smiled at her. "Actually, I was. I got there really late, when almost everyone had gone home."

"I stayed pretty late myself," she said. "We must have just missed each other."

"It's best to keep the story simple and easy to remember," I said. "We met on New Year's Eve, we fell for each other fast and hard, I proposed last week, and you accepted."

"Too simple," Ava said. "Our story needs to sound like a whirlwind romance, not a business summary. We should brainstorm the details together."

"What kind of details?" I asked.

"The kind of things people remember about meeting the love of their life."

I raised an eyebrow at her. "Are you asking me to come up with sappy shit? Because if so, you're talking to the wrong guy."

"It doesn't have to be sappy," she said. "The details that make our backstory sound real could be funny, or personal. What do you remember about major turning points in your life, like the day you graduated from college, or the day you started your business?"

I shrugged. "Not much. I'm not a details man."

"How about this?" she said. "We met at Cara's party. We got into a conversation about our favorite movies, and although we'd just met, we felt as if we'd known each other forever. At the end of the evening, when it was time for me to leave, you asked me to have dinner with you at Blacktail the following night, and I agreed."

"Of course you did," I said. "According to your story, I'd just spent the evening charming your panties off."

She gave me an exasperated look. "Put your oversized ego on hold and let me finish. The next day—New Year's Day—felt like the longest day ever, because we were both counting the minutes until eight o'clock, when we would see each other again. When we met at Blacktail, we both ordered steak and shared a plate of fries. You had a glass of Scotch, and I had a martini."

"I get where you're going," I said. "You're basing the story on our actual dinner."

"It's easier to remember if we stay close to the truth," she said. "Over dinner, the hours flew by. We talked about everything under the sun, neither of us wanting the evening to end, until the restaurant was about to close for the night. After we left Blacktail, you walked me to the subway. It was a mild night, and a few scattered snowflakes were drifting in the air around us when you kissed me for the first time, just outside the Broad Street station."

"Are you done?"

"I am," she said. "What do you think of my story?"

"It sounds like a chick flick."

She rolled her eyes. "It sounds romantic, which is more believable than your slam-bam version of how we supposedly fell in love."

"Fine," I said. "We'll go with your version. Now that we've resolved that, let's move on to the wedding plans. Getting married at the Southampton estate means that we won't have to search for a venue, and my father will be pleased that we want to be married there. However, Southampton also means that we have to deal with Veronica."

Ava nodded. "Cara's told me how difficult your stepmother can be. We definitely need to make sure we're on the same page before talking wedding plans with her."

"I've thought it through," I said. "We should keep the ceremony simple."

"I agree. Cara will be my maid of honor, and I assume Jack will be your best man. We can use whoever your family would prefer as a reverend or priest; we don't need a full bridal party, and I don't need anyone to walk me down the aisle."

I picked up my wineglass, relaxed against my chair, and sipped the Barolo. So far, this discussion was going well. Aside from her embellishments to our backstory, Ava had agreed with everything I'd suggested.

"Back to Veronica," I said. "The best way to deal with my stepmother is to let her have her way whenever it doesn't interfere with what we want."

Ava's eyes twinkled with humor. "A good recipe for dealing with anyone."

"I expect Veronica to push for a large bridal party," I said.

"Then we'll push back."

"She'll want to oversee the guest list and the reception," I said. "The easiest way through all of it is to let her take charge."

"That may be the easiest way," Ava said. "But not the best."

"Why not?"

She scrunched up her face at me. "Appearances, of course."

"My stepmother's the queen of appearances. She'll invite her socialite friends; she'll jump at the opportunity to impress them, and to that end, she'll make sure the reception is stunning and the food excellent."

"That's not what I meant by appearances," Ava said.

"Then what the hell did you mean?"

She leveled me with a look. "Think like a woman, Ronan—you've certainly slept with enough of them. Consider the symbolism of what you've just proposed."

"What I've proposed makes perfect sense," I said. "A simple wedding that won't require a ton of time to set up."

"What you've proposed is a one-way street to disaster. We need to be involved—"

Annoyed by her resistance, I cut her off. "I have a multimillion-dollar business to run. Maybe your busy schedule allows time to taste twenty kinds of cake, but mine doesn't."

Her delicate nostrils flared. "Then you'll have to make time."

"Give me one good reason."

"I was about to, when you interrupted me."

"Go ahead," I said. "Enlighten me."

"I'll try," she said. "Although I doubt that shining light on the testosterone-laced rock you call your brain can produce anything resembling enlightenment."

My irritation grew. "Try logic. Although that's clearly an alien concept to you, and every other woman on the planet."

She glared at me. "Women are every bit as logical as men."

"I disagree."

"You would. Because you're a male chauvinist pig. A species that only thinks in straight lines. Women can juggle multiple thoughts at once. We think holistically."

"That's new-age bullshit."

"Actually, it's science. Google it."

With effort, I contained my temper. "I have better things to do with my time. Tell me why you don't want to let Veronica have her way with the reception."

"Letting your stepmother take control will only raise her suspicions," Ava said. "If we don't show interest and involvement in planning every detail of what's supposed to be our big day, we might as well paint 'fake marriage' across our foreheads."

My gut twisted. How could I not have seen this coming? I'd been so focused on the logistics of pulling a wedding together in six weeks, I hadn't stopped to consider how my attempts to streamline that process might appear to others—especially Veronica, who would leap at any opportunity to question my motives. As much as I hated to admit it, Ava was right.

"I see your point," I said.

Ava sipped her wine. "I hope you do. Allowing Veronica to manage our wedding is like waving a large red flag at a bull that's already planted its horns in your ass."

*Fuck my life.*

I slumped back in my chair and resigned myself to spending the next six weeks tasting cakes, faking interest in floral arrangements, and dealing with my bitch of a stepmother. What did it even matter? To save my company, I'd already signed away my sex life and committed to two years of living with a woman I barely knew. At this point, my life could hardly get worse.

"Bring on the wedding bullshit," I said. "I'll do my best to play the part."

Surprise flashed across Ava's face. "Are you agreeing with me?"

"I am. I'd hoped to spare you from battling with Veronica over the wedding arrangements, but after the points you raised, I don't see any way of dodging that fight. There's too much on the line to risk fucking this up."

Ava's expression softened. "I appreciate that you were trying to make things easier for me."

"It's the least I can do," I said. "Depending on the day, coping with my stepmother can be anywhere between hellish and suicidal."

"Don't worry about me," she said. "I've dealt with my share of difficult people. If we work together, we can get through this. In any case, there's no avoiding Veronica."

"No," I said. "Unfortunately, there isn't."

# 13

## RONAN

That weekend, I woke at ten o'clock on Saturday morning with a sense of well-being that had been absent from my life in recent months. The previous night, I had told my father about my engagement and secured his permission to get married on the Southampton estate, and after that conversation ended, I'd decided to give myself a day off. With my marriage plans on schedule, and my finances on track toward a successful resolution, I deserved a break.

I sat up in bed, swung my feet to the floor, and headed for the bathroom. As I emptied my bladder, splashed water on my face, and brushed my teeth, I anticipated the laid-back day that stretched before me.

I'd fix myself a king-sized breakfast and watch the news. Then I'd play my favorite video game for an hour or two. In the afternoon, I'd work out and maybe give Jack a call to see if he wanted to meet for drinks later tonight. I might have signed away my sex life, but I could still look—and drink a Scotch or two with my best friend.

After leaving the bathroom, I put on sweat pants and a T-shirt and headed toward the kitchen. When I reached the living room, Ava was sitting on the couch with a cup of coffee in her hand, watching CNN. Casually dressed in dark jeans and a white blouse, her face was free of makeup, but she still looked good. Most women couldn't pull off the bare-faced look, but with her full lips, delicate features, and dark, long-lashed eyes, Ava was one of the few who could.

When she saw me, she reached for the remote and muted the television. "Good morning," she said. "There's fresh coffee if you want it."

"Thanks," I said. "I'll take you up on that."

I stepped into the kitchen, poured myself a cup of coffee, and added a splash of half-and-half before I joined Ava in the living room. Breakfast could wait until I updated her on last night's conversation with my father.

"Dad finally called me back last night," I said.

"How did it go?" she asked.

I sat down in my armchair. "As expected. I told him about our engagement and that we want to get married in Southampton on May seventh. He was fine with everything."

"No cross-examination?" Ava said.

"Dad doesn't do that kind of thing. He's always been too focused on his work to take much interest in any of his three children—unless one of us screws up or embarrasses him in some way."

Ava nodded. "Cara once told me that your father's never gone to a show of her paintings, which kind of shocked me. I don't have many memories of my parents, but my grandparents were always there for me."

I almost told her how lucky she was, but then I stopped myself. While her grandparents sounded a hell of a lot better than Dad and Veronica, Ava's life hadn't been easy, and I didn't want to sound like a whiny jerk.

"In our family, Veronica's the cross-examiner," I said. "Although my father did ask a few questions about your background."

Ava's lips quirked. "My nonexistent pedigree, you mean."

I sipped my coffee. "It's true that Dad's a snob. But your Harvard degree made a positive impression on him, as did the fact that you run your own business."

"When do he and Veronica expect to meet me?"

"He suggested a family dinner next week," I said. "Veronica will call to set a date."

"How formal should I expect this dinner to be?" Ava asked.

I shrugged. "I usually wear a jacket but skip the tie. I'm sure whatever you want to wear will be fine."

She looked amused. "Men. When it comes to fashion advice, you're about as useful as a phone without a signal."

I gave her a suggestive look. "I'm an expert on undergarments—but I don't expect you want my help choosing panties."

"Pig," she said mildly. "Although right now you look more like a sleepy hedgehog."

I rubbed my jawline, which did need a trim. "Hedgehog?"

"It's not your stubble," she said. "It's your hair, which is spiked out on one side and doing a bizarre wave thing on the other. If you dyed it lavender, you could crash a Halloween party as Kelly Osbourne."

I laughed. "That'll be the day."

Just then, the door phone buzzed.

"That must be Cara," Ava said. "We have lunch plans—although I didn't expect her this early."

I rested my mug on the coffee table, got up from my chair, stepped into the foyer, and picked up the receiver to tell the doorman to send my sister up.

But when I did, the phone emitted a burst of static, followed by a familiar voice that sent a chill down my spine.

"Good morning, darling. I've stopped by for a quick visit. See you in a minute."

With difficulty, I restrained the impulse to tell Veronica to go fuck herself. Instead, when she returned the phone to the doorman, I told him to send her up. What choice did I have? As usual, my stepmother had successfully seized control.

I hung up the receiver and raced back to the living room to warn Ava. "It's not Cara. It's Veronica, and she'll be here within seconds."

Calmly, Ava set down her mug on the coffee table and got to her feet. "Cara predicted that Veronica would drop in on us," she said. "She's shown up sooner than we expected, but we'll be fine. Get the door when she arrives, and stall her for a minute or so while I check the bedrooms to make sure everything looks OK."

And with that, she disappeared into the master suite.

I dashed into the half bath off the foyer and checked out my reflection in the mirror, which confirmed that my hair was as fucked up as Ava had said it was. After splashing water over my hair and face, I grabbed a hand towel and sopped up the excess, before slicking back my hair with my fingers.

A knock at the door announced my stepmother's arrival.

"Coming!" I yelled as I strode back to the living area and looked around for Ava. Where was she, and what the hell was she doing? We were out of time.

Just then, she emerged from her bedroom.

"All good?" I asked.

She gave me a thumbs-up. "Bring it on."

## 14

### AVA

When Ronan opened the door and Veronica stepped inside, I was struck by her beauty but also by something that Cara's family photos hadn't revealed—the subtle arrogance that emanated from her like a poison invisible to the eye but palpable in her presence.

Tall and statuesque, with dark eyes, classic features, and black hair swept back from her face in a sleek chignon, Veronica was elegantly dressed in a taupe silk pantsuit that flattered her well-maintained figure. Diamonds glittered at her ears, a Hermès scarf was knotted loosely around her neck, and a tan Birkin hung from her shoulder. Although I knew that Veronica was well into her fifties, she didn't look a day over forty, and as I moved to Ronan's side to greet her, I felt dingy and unkempt in my casual blouse and jeans and wished that I'd had time to apply a dash of makeup.

"You must be Ava," she said, flashing a gleaming smile as she looked me up and down.

"Allow me," Ronan said. "Veronica, I'd like to introduce my fiancée, Ava Walker. Ava, this is my stepmother, Veronica Kingsley."

Veronica sighed. "Ronan, Ronan. Always so formal. You'd never know that I've been his mother since he was seven years old." She placed a manicured hand on my arm. "Ever since Carter told me the happy news last night, I've been dying to meet you. And then it occurred to me that I needed to stop by Bergdorf's and pick up the dress I've chosen for the Met gala. So here I am, killing two birds with one stone." She tittered at her joke, before turning back to Ronan. "She's lovely, Ronan. Where on earth did you find her? Not in one of your usual whiskey dens, I imagine."

I felt Ronan stiffen beside me. "Ronan and I met at Cara's New Year's party," I said, giving Veronica my best fake smile. "But won't you come in and sit down? Let me get you a cup of coffee—or something else to drink, if you prefer."

"Perhaps a glass of mineral water," Veronica said.

"I'll get it," Ronan said and gestured toward the living room. "Go ahead and sit down—I'll join you in a moment."

When Veronica entered the living room, she eyed the colorful arrangement of roses and Peruvian lilies that I had placed on one of the end tables that flanked the couch.

"I see that you've already made a few changes to Ronan's apartment," she said as she seated herself in his favorite armchair. "Which is all to the good. Like his father, my stepson has no interest in decorating."

It was her third dig at Ronan in as many minutes. No wonder my husband-to-be avoided his stepmother like an infectious disease. Given his quick temper, Veronica's bitchy little barbs probably set him off like a rocket.

"Ronan may not be into decorating, but he has fabulous taste," I said as I held up my left hand to show off my ring. She'd been darting glances at it since she walked through the door, and I meant to give her a good look. "He couldn't have chosen a more beautiful engagement ring."

She pursed her lips. "Harry Winston never disappoints. The oval shape suits your hand, and the micropavé frame and band are stunning. But you didn't choose it yourself?"

"Ronan surprised me with it," I said as I sat down on the couch. "It was the most romantic moment of my life."

"How sweet," Veronica said lightly. "But let's talk about you. The woman who finally convinced my playboy stepson to settle down. I'm simply consumed with curiosity, and although my husband is a financial wizard, the man is useless when it comes to passing on any information that doesn't fit into a spreadsheet. After Carter's conversation with Ronan last night, all the man could tell me is that you roomed with Cara at Harvard, and you run your own floral-design business in Brooklyn."

"Cara and I became friends during freshman year," I said. "We were roommates for the rest of college, and since we both live in New York, we've been fortunate to be able to keep up our friendship."

"And you and Ronan met at New Year's?"

Just then, Ronan returned from the kitchen with a glass of mineral water, which he handed to Veronica.

"We did," he said as he sat down on the couch beside me. "And when I realized what a treasure I'd stumbled upon, I seized the moment. After Cara's party ended, I walked Ava to the subway and asked her to have dinner with me the following night."

I gave Ronan an appreciative look and placed my hand over his, grateful that he was sticking with the backstory we'd discussed. As long as we kept our story consistent, we'd be fine. Thanks to the work Cara and I had done staging the apartment, nothing but our own words or actions could give us away.

"Such a romantic story," Veronica said airily. "Love at first sight. But now that the two of you have set a date, there are a few things we need to discuss."

"I'd prefer to go over our wedding plans when the entire family is present," Ronan said. His deep voice was calm, but I sensed his tension. "Dad suggested that we all get together for dinner in the coming week. We can deal with the wedding then."

Veronica sipped her water before dropping her bomb. "I'm not talking about your wedding, darling."

"Then what are you talking about?" he said.

She sighed. "You'll accuse me of meddling," she said. "You always do."

Ronan leveled her with a look. "Since when has that stopped you?"

Veronica gave me an exasperated look. "See what I have to deal with? Even as a child, he was always difficult."

"Enough about my childhood," Ronan said. "What do you want to discuss?"

Her voice dripped with fake sweetness. "Your engagement party, darling. I plan on handling it myself."

# 15

## AVA

"Engagement party?" Ronan said. "What engagement party?"

"The engagement party your father and I are throwing for you and Ava, which is the reason I made time to drop by today."

Although Ronan's expression was impassive, I could feel him vibrating with annoyance. Clearly, Veronica's announcement had taken him by surprise. And over the past two weeks, I'd learned that my husband-to-be wasn't a man who responded well to surprises—especially surprises that stole time away from his work.

So before Ronan could stick his foot in his mouth, I did what needed to be done—the only thing that could be done.

"That's very generous of you and Carter," I said, forcing my lips into a smile as I squeezed Ronan's hand in a desperate signal I hoped he would understand. "And we'd love to celebrate our engagement with you. But are you sure that you want to go to so much trouble for us? By hosting our wedding, you're already doing more than enough."

"Consider it an early wedding gift," Veronica said. Her voice took on an edge. "You wouldn't understand this, Ava, but the Kingsley family has a reputation to uphold. Your wedding may be rushed—no doubt for the usual reasons—but that's no excuse for Ronan to disregard his social obligations."

As I processed what I'd just heard, my blood heated. I'd done my best to think of everything. I'd prepared myself to face suspicion, even hostility. But I'd completely failed to consider the possibility that Veronica would think that Ronan and I were rushing to the altar because I was knocked up or that I had deliberately gotten pregnant to trap Ronan into marriage.

Furious, I opened my mouth to defend myself.

But before I could speak, my common sense reasserted itself. Regardless of my feelings, I needed to take this one for the team. Veronica was looking for an explanation of why Ronan and I were fast-tracking our marriage, and believing I was pregnant was preferable to other directions her imagination might travel in—like the truth.

So I pressed my lips together, suppressed my anger, and swallowed my injured pride.

The bitch shot me another of her toothpaste-commercial smiles. "You're blushing," she said teasingly. "I've guessed right, haven't I?"

It was then that Ronan surprised me. "Ava's not pregnant," he said evenly.

Veronica raised an arched brow. "Really?"

Ronan glared at her. "Really. So stop suggesting that my fiancée and future wife is a gold digger. It's insulting, not to mention untrue."

"As usual, you're overreacting," Veronica said. "I suggested no such thing. I merely voiced what everyone will think, due to the abruptness of your engagement and wedding."

Ronan's lips tightened. "I don't give a shit what people think. Here's the reality. Ava and I are adults, we know what we want, and once we decided to build a life together, neither of us saw any point in delaying our marriage."

His protectiveness moved me, and I couldn't resist adding a twist of my own. "But don't worry, Veronica—you'll be a grandmother soon. After Ronan and I enjoy a year or two as newlyweds, we hope to start a family."

Ronan's hand twitched beneath mine, but his voice remained steady. "Long engagements are old-fashioned. You know I've never been one to concern myself with silly conventions."

Veronica released a brittle laugh. "I'm well aware of your lack of interest in doing things properly, darling—but perhaps I've spoiled you by taking care of such matters for you. In any case, one convention that will be observed is an engagement party in Southampton for you and Ava."

"Very well," Ronan said. "What date have you and my father chosen?"

"Two weeks from today."

"We'll add it to our calendar," he said. "What do you need from us?"

"Only your presence and the names of any people you and Ava want to invite," Veronica said. "I'll take care of everything else."

"Is there anything I can do to help?" I asked. "I have a lot of event-planning experience."

"I doubt your experience extends to this kind of event," Veronica said. She rested her half-empty water glass on the coffee table and glanced at her wristwatch. "Now that that's settled, I should be running along," she said as she stood and slung her Birkin over her shoulder. "I'd prefer not to be late for my appointment at Bergdorf's."

Ronan and I stood with her, and as she headed toward the foyer, I sensed and shared his relief that she was leaving.

But then she stopped and turned to us. "I nearly forgot," she said. "Before I go, Ronan, show me what you've done with Cara's paintings. She mentioned that you bought half a dozen pieces from her last show."

*Here we go.*

Just as Cara had predicted, Veronica was hell-bent on nosing through our apartment—and she'd provided an impeccable pretext. Fortunately, thanks to Cara, I was prepared.

"The smaller paintings are in here," I said, leading the way to my room. "This room used to be Ronan's guest bedroom, but we've turned it into an office and TV room for me."

Veronica followed me into the room, with Ronan behind her.

"Cara's paintings look wonderful on the green you chose for the walls," she said. "Although she hasn't found much success as a painter, I think she's very talented."

"I agree," I said. "Cara's paintings are unique and original, and I just know that someday she'll be famous."

Veronica's gaze drifted over the room's furnishings and stopped on my grandmother's desk. "You should get rid of that old desk. It looks cheap, and it clashes with the tone of the room."

"It may not be an ideal match with the other furniture," I said, bristling at her dismissal of the most precious object I owned. "But it belonged to my grandmother, and I love it."

"It's hardly an heirloom," Veronica said, wrinkling her nose. "If you can't bring yourself to throw it away, why not store it? Now, where are the rest of the paintings?"

"In the master," Ronan said. "Follow me."

Veronica and I trailed him into the master suite, where she admired Cara's paintings, while Ronan took in the last-minute adjustments I'd made before his stepmother's arrival. A lacy black brassiere peeked from beneath the rumpled sheets of his unmade bed, and matching panties lay on the floor beside the bed.

As I'd expected she might, Veronica excused herself to use the bathroom, which I felt certain was an excuse to go through its contents.

When the door closed behind her, Ronan stepped just behind me.

"Nice touch with the underwear," he said in a low voice against my ear. "My bed looks like it's seen some serious action."

"That's the idea," I whispered back, trying to remain composed. With Ronan standing so close to me that his breath caressed my neck, and Veronica in the next room, no doubt inspecting my makeup and tampons, I'd never been less at ease.

What was wrong with me? How had I ever thought myself capable of handling this situation? Maybe I'd escaped my financial problems, but in doing so, I'd created a host of new problems that I didn't even begin to know how to deal with.

A posh engagement party with the Southampton elite—the kind of people I was accustomed to working for, not socializing with.

A hostile monster-in-law.

And a fake husband-to-be who, despite my best efforts, I found increasingly attractive. I only hoped that my loose-fitting blouse concealed the fact that his proximity had brought my nipples to full attention. How could I be so turned on by a man I didn't get along with half of the time and who was also a total man-whore? Was I that starved for sex?

It was completely irrational—but I couldn't deny that whenever Ronan accidentally touched me or came near me, my body lit up like a goddamned disco ball.

The only saving grace was that he wasn't into me in that way, which made my attraction to him irrelevant. Hopefully, with time I would get over it. I stepped away from him and forced myself to focus, just as the sound of a flushing toilet announced Veronica's imminent return. Moments later, she emerged from the dressing area and bathroom that was supposedly mine.

"Thank you, darlings," she said breezily. "Now, I really must get on with my day. In any case, you two lovebirds surely have your own plans, which I've interrupted for too long already."

We followed her from the master suite into the living area, where she turned toward the foyer and the door.

"I'll be in touch," she said as Ronan opened the door for her. "And Ava—before the party, do something about your hands. We can't have Ronan's fiancée show up looking like a farmer."

I resisted the urge to slap her. "Of course," I said. "Since my work makes it impossible to maintain a manicure, I always get one before events."

"Perfect," she said. "Toodles, darlings—and don't worry about a thing. Just send me the names of anyone you want to invite by tomorrow night, and I'll make sure they receive an invitation."

"We'll do that," Ronan said.

"Then I'm off," she said. With a wave and a final flash of teeth, she disappeared into the elevator.

After Ronan closed the door behind her, he turned to face me.

"Thank you for that," he said. "You handled her beautifully."

"I don't know about that. But I did the best I could."

"My stepmother's a piece of work. No one could have done better."

Warmed by his praise, I smiled at him. "You were pretty amazing yourself."

He shot me a mischievous grin. "What I am is lucky. After your performance today, I know we can do this. We'll have to go a few more rounds with Veronica, but eventually, she'll be forced to give up and accept that our fake relationship is real."

"You have more faith in my acting skills than I do," I said. "But I hope you're right."

"I know I'm right," he said.

And then, for the second time in the past half hour, he surprised me by saying the last thing I expected to hear.

"The two of us make a great team."

# 16

## AVA

"I can't believe the engagement party is tomorrow," I said to Mimi. "I'm totally dreading it."

My friend put down her fork and looked across the table at me. "You and Ronan are going to be fine," she said. "Didn't you just say that things have been going better between the two of you?"

I'd asked her to meet me for lunch at Veselka, an East Village diner that served a mixture of classic diner fare and Ukrainian specialties, because with the party bearing down on me, I needed to bolster my spirits and calm my nerves, both of which Mimi's presence usually did for me.

"For the most part, they have," I said. "We haven't been arguing—well, at least not about anything important."

Mimi pushed a tendril of curly red hair away from her face. "You and Ronan are both strong personalities," she said. "You can't expect to agree about everything. What's important is establishing friendship, rapport, and agreement about the big stuff. That's what will carry you through the next two years."

"I do feel like we're becoming friends," I said. "When I first moved in, he spent so much time at work that I felt like I was living alone. But over the past two weeks since we announced our engagement, he's been spending more time at the apartment. Sometimes he works out or spends the evening in his home office—but sometimes we make dinner together and watch a movie. Like me, he loves classic Hollywood movies, although the other night, when we watched *Notorious*, he gave me hell for drooling over Cary Grant."

Mimi sighed. "What woman hasn't drooled over Cary Grant? He's only the sexiest, most gorgeous man to ever walk the face of the earth."

"When I said just that, Ronan called him an overrated dandy," I said. "Although I eventually forced him to acknowledge that Cary had serious acting chops."

"Typical male jealousy," Mimi said, her eyes twinkling. "Although your fake husband-to-be has no need to be jealous of any man. He's smoking hot."

"He's all that, and then some—which is becoming a problem."

Mimi furrowed her brow. "What do you mean? Has Ronan broken your agreement in some way?"

"No—not at all," I said. "He's been great. Like I said, we're becoming friends. The problem is me."

She gave me a long, penetrating look before she spoke. "You're attracted to him, aren't you?"

"I am," I confessed. "I shouldn't be, and I know better. But none of that changes the fact that when he touches me by accident, or stands near me when we're making dinner together, I totally want to tear his clothes off."

"Then why don't you?" Mimi said. "It's not as though you'd be breaking your agreement. Neither of you can have sex with other people, but there's nothing in your agreement about getting it on with each other."

"Too risky. Besides, he's not into me in that way. I'm not the type of woman he's attracted to. Cara told me once that Ronan likes blondes with big tits, which is pretty much the polar opposite of me."

"You're a beautiful woman," Mimi said. "If you put the moves on Ronan, he won't turn you down."

"Maybe not. But that would only create a bigger mess."

"How so?"

"By blurring the boundaries of our arrangement. Having sex with Ronan would confuse everything."

"It could. But it doesn't have to."

"I disagree."

She leveled me with a look. "Communication is everything, Ava. You and Ronan are free to change your arrangement in any way you like, as long as you're honest with each other. I may not be a fan of commitment—but open communication is the key to all successful relationships, whether those relationships are long or short."

"Maybe you're right, but I've never experienced anything like this. You know I've always been a relationship kind of girl."

"You know my feelings on that topic," Mimi said. "Sex is a simple human need—why complicate it?"

"I don't know. Maybe because sex has never felt simple to me. Maybe because my dream is to find Mr. Right and build a life and a family together."

"One thing's for sure," Mimi said. "Ronan's no Mr. Right. He's a Mr. Right Now."

"Exactly," I said. "If I did have sex with him, what if that led to feelings? What if I started falling for him? It's not like I could just run the other way—not when we've made a two-year commitment to each other."

Mimi rummaged in her purse, pulled out a long, silver e-cigarette that no doubt contained some form of marijuana, and took an extended drag on it before she responded.

"I understand your hesitation," she said. "You're torn between fear and attraction."

"That's just it. What do you think I should do?"

"What I think doesn't matter," she said, before taking another drag on her e-cigarette. "You have to do what's right for you—and you also need to chill the fuck out. You're practically vibrating right now. You shouldn't stress yourself out by overthinking this."

I sighed. "I'm definitely guilty of overthinking this."

"You don't have to make a decision today. Just remember that you and Ronan are free adults. Whatever you do—or don't do—is between the two of you. But sex doesn't have to turn into a relationship. Sometimes, sex can be just sex."

"I don't know," I said. "Sex with Ronan seems risky to me. And with any luck, my insane attraction to him will pass with time."

"Or not," Mimi said, giving me a mischievous look. "The most effective way to relieve an itch is to scratch it, you know."

I rolled my eyes. "You're too much. But perhaps I'll consider taking your advice—about two years from now."

## 17

RONAN

When the day of the engagement party arrived, Ava spent the morning getting a manicure and pedicure, while I did my best to relax by working out and then playing my favorite video game.

After Ava returned, I made us a light lunch, before we separated to get ready. With characteristic thoroughness, Veronica had arranged for my father's chauffeur to pick us up in his limo, which simplified getting to and from Southampton. Thankfully, my stepmother hadn't pressed us to stay overnight.

As I looked through my ties to choose one that would complement my dark-gray suit, I remembered that Ava had told me she would be wearing a red dress. Should I wear a red tie—or would that be too "matchy-matchy," as Cara would say? After some deliberation, I selected a silver Brioni tie with a subtle geometric texture. After knotting it around my neck, I adjusted my collar, stepped in front of the mirror, and decided that I'd made the right choice. The sheen of the tie looked good with my white shirt and gray suit, and with Ava in red, the two of us would make a fine-looking couple.

After finishing my preparations, I went into the kitchen to get a glass of water. As I filled a tumbler with Evian, I heard a door open. I was just taking my first sip of water when Ava entered the kitchen.

"Wow," I said as she stepped toward me and did a little twirl. "You're stunning."

It was no less than the truth. The scarlet fabric of her sleeveless, floor-length dress shimmered against her curves. The neckline of her dress bared one slender shoulder, and a thigh-high slit on the opposite side revealed flashes of long, shapely leg. The ring I'd given her glittered on her left hand, and diamond solitaires gleamed against her ears. Her dark, wavy hair was pulled back into a sleek chignon, but she'd allowed a few tendrils to escape around her face in ways that were sexy as hell. In her right hand, she carried a star-shaped clutch bag covered with sparkling beads and crystals that matched the scarlet of her dress. What was she wearing beneath it? In response to that thought, my cock hardened. I forced my mind to boner-killing thoughts, visualizing the least attractive women I could think of naked.

Which wasn't easy with Ava standing right in front of me, not when I wanted to seize her and peel that dress off her one inch at a time.

But tonight wasn't about pleasure. I had a job to do. At the thought of what blowing up my fake marriage would mean for my business, the pressure in my cock began to recede.

"Thank you," Ava said. She gave me an uncharacteristically shy half smile. "Doing myself up like this was nothing short of an epic production, but I love the dress, purse, and heels that Cara and I chose together—not to mention the earrings."

"My sister knows her stuff," I said, shifting the left side of my jacket to conceal the remainder of my not-so-little problem. "You look amazing."

"I'm relieved that you like it," she said. "You paid for it, after all."

"How much?"

"The whole ensemble, including the earrings? Nearly twenty grand."

"Worth every penny," I said, meaning it. "You look like a fire princess."

She laughed. "Cinderella is more like it—but thank you. Between the dress, the four-inch heels, and the diamonds, I feel like a princess."

With my cock now under control, I tossed back the rest of my water and then put the glass down on the counter before holding out my arm to Ava. "My father's driver will be outside any minute, if he isn't already there. Shall we?"

She took my arm. "Let's do it."

## 18

### AVA

Since early April was off-season for the Hamptons, our afternoon drive to Southampton took just over two hours, less than half the time it could take during the summer months. When the limo turned into the wide gravel driveway of the estate, passed the security gate, and proceeded down a long, tree-lined driveway toward a four-story, shingle-sided mansion, it was half past five, and the late-afternoon sun cast a warm glow over the landscape.

I couldn't help staring. Southampton real estate was among the most expensive in the United States, and based on what the view from the car's windows, Ronan's family owned a massive chunk of it.

Ronan gestured to the right. "The tennis court and guest house are over there," he said, pointing toward a second shingle-sided building that looked like another mansion. "The beach is just beyond the main house."

The driveway widened into a spacious parking court, where I noticed several delivery vehicles, their presence no doubt connected to tonight's party. The driver stopped in front of the house, before getting out and opening the door. Ronan got out first and then helped me out of the car. In his perfectly fitted suit, he was impossibly handsome, and as he guided me from the car to the ground, a twinge of arousal shot through me. Between the limousine ride, the fairy-tale beauty of the setting, and Ronan's attentiveness, it felt as if I'd stepped into one of the romantic movies I loved. Today was so unlike my everyday life, it was almost an out-of-body experience.

"It's warm for early April," he said. "Would you like to see the beach before we go inside?"

"I'd love to," I said. "But in the heels I'm wearing, I don't dare to set foot on the beach. If I show up for this party with sand-covered feet, Veronica will murder both of us."

"I have a solution," he said. "Hold on to my arm."

Carefully, he guided me across the manicured lawn to the right of the house as the salty sea air filled my nostrils. At the corner of the house, we turned left and walked up several steps onto a broad porch that faced the water. As I turned toward the ocean, a light breeze stirred my hair, and the sound of crashing surf reached my ears. Before us, a broad strip of lawn gave way to dunes carpeted with mounds of rosa rugosa bushes that stretched to a pristine expanse of sand and the ocean beyond.

"It's beautiful," I said. "No wonder your father and Veronica prefer to spend most of their time here."

"I spent summers here when I was a kid," he said.

"What was that like?" I asked. He rarely spoke about his childhood, but I knew from Cara that from the time she and Ronan reached adolescence, they had avoided spending much time with their father and stepmother.

"Between Dad's busy work schedule and the amount of entertaining he and Veronica do, it could get monotonous for a kid," he said. "But the Mortons were good to me. Evelyn never minded when I trailed her around the house or hung out in the kitchen. She always kept my favorite peanut-butter cookies on hand. And Alfred taught me to ride my first bicycle."

"Will I have a chance to meet them tonight?"

From conversations with Cara and Ronan, I knew that Alfred Morton and his wife, Evelyn, were the butler and housekeeper—together, they had managed the estate and its staff for decades. Childless themselves, in some ways the Mortons had parented Cara and Ronan more than their father and stepmother had.

"We'll find an opportunity," Ronan said. "I think of Alfred and Evelyn as family, and I never come here without making time to see them." He looked out at the ocean. "Aside from spending time with them, the other thing I enjoyed about summers here was being outside. I liked my tennis and sailing lessons—especially sailing."

"I don't really know how to sail," I said. "But during college, I sailed a few times with a friend whose parents had a house in Woods Hole."

"Did you enjoy it?" he asked.

"I loved being on the water, although I didn't have a clue how to manage the boat. I just yanked on whatever rope my friend told me to pull."

"Then we'll make time to go for a sail this summer," he said. "We can take my father's boat—or I can rent one."

Surprised and pleased by his offer, I squeezed his arm. "I'd like that."

Just then, a door opened, and Veronica emerged, looking flawless in a cream-colored, floor-length sheath dress and matching heels. A tall, distinguished-looking man wearing a navy-blue jacket and tan trousers followed her, and I immediately recognized him as Carter Kingsley, Ronan and Cara's father. Aside from Carter's dark eyes, silver-streaked hair, and the creases around his eyes and mouth, Ronan strongly resembled his father.

"For goodness sake, Ronan," Veronica said. "What were you thinking, dragging Ava out here? She'll catch her death of cold."

Did Ronan's stepmother ever miss an opportunity to put him down? If she did, I hadn't witnessed it yet.

"I'm fine," I said. "It's a warm evening, and it's my fault that we're outside. We came here because I asked Ronan to show me the view."

Veronica shook her head disapprovingly before turning to her husband. "Carter, darling, why don't you take Ava and Ronan to the second-floor sitting room? I need to keep an eye on the staff and caterers."

"I'll do that," Carter said, in a voice that reminded me of Ronan's. As Veronica disappeared into the house, he held out his hand to me. "Welcome to our home, Ava. I'm delighted to finally meet you."

I shook his hand. "It's great to meet you too."

After releasing me, Carter shook Ronan's hand, clapped his son on the back, and gave me a charming smile as his gaze traveled over my body in a way that made me uncomfortable. "You didn't tell me how beautiful your fiancée is, Ronan. Now that I've seen her for myself, I understand why your bachelor days have come to an end."

"Ava's unique," Ronan said as we followed Carter inside. "From the day we met, I knew she was the woman I wanted to marry."

Carter led us down a wide, well-lit hallway, the walls of which were lined with oil paintings. Through an open door, I caught a glimpse of a room bustling with caterers and staff that appeared to be the estate's kitchen and a second room in which two floral designers were putting finishing touches on several arrangements. After leading us up a flight of stairs and stepping into a second hallway, Carter paused and gestured toward the entrance of a ballroom-sized space to his right.

"The party will be here—in the oceanside room," he said to me, before turning left and leading us into a smaller sitting room.

Before following him, I paused to glance inside the space where the party would be held, and caught a glimpse of tall, arched windows overlooking the ocean. Veronica stood before the windows, speaking with a group of black-suited caterers, no doubt giving them their instructions for the evening.

When I stepped into the sitting room, it turned out to be a smaller, more intimate cousin of the oceanside room, with high ceilings and a single arched window overlooking the water.

"Sit here," Carter said to Ronan and me, indicating a couch that faced the window. "Can I get either of you a drink?"

"I wouldn't say no to a Scotch," Ronan said. "Are you still drinking Laphroaig?"

"The eighteen-year?" Carter said. "It's my evening tipple. Alfred orders it for me by the case."

"I'll have a glass of that," Ronan said as the two of us sat down on the couch.

Carter pressed a button on the wall before sitting in an armchair across from us.

"What would you like to drink, Ava?" he said.

"Just a glass of water, thank you," I said. If I was going to survive this party, I needed to keep my wits about me.

Carter gave me a flirtatious look. "Shouldn't we raise a glass to your engagement?"

Ronan took my hand and squeezed it. "Have a glass of Laphroaig," he said. "Trust me, you'll like it."

Maybe a sip of liquid courage would help me relax. So far, Ronan's father had been pleasant enough, but the way he looked at me had a distinctly sexual undertone, which turned my stomach. How could he look at his son's fiancée in that way?

"OK," I said. "I'll try it."

Just then, a young man in a dark suit entered the room.

"What can I get for you, Mr. Kingsley?" he said.

"Three glasses of Laphroaig on the rocks," Carter said. "Thank you, James." The young man nodded in acknowledgment before exiting the room.

I glanced around the space, taking in the panes of the arched window and the elaborate molding that traced the line between walls and ceiling. Both confirmed my initial impression, based on the house's traditional exterior, that it had been built in the early twentieth century. But the interior had been completely redone in a modernist style, with white walls and furniture; dark hardwood floors; and flowing, translucent white drapes. The only color in the room came from several floor vases that looked like they belonged in a museum. In a minimal, antiseptic way, the room was beautiful—but it felt more like a posh hotel than a home. Footsteps and voices echoed from the hallway outside, reminding me that the engagement party I dreaded was only minutes away.

"So, Ava," Carter said, "before our guests arrive, tell me a little about yourself. Ronan and Cara have told me that you were Cara's roommate at Harvard, but I don't recall meeting you."

"That's because you haven't, Mr. Kingsley," I said. "Today is the first time we've met."

"Call me Carter," he said smoothly. "And we must have met, because I met all of Cara's roommates during her graduation week at Harvard."

"I didn't attend most of the graduation events," I said. "My grandparents—the last of my family—died during my college years, and graduations are family affairs."

"That explains it," Carter said with an air of satisfaction. "I never forget a pretty face—and I would certainly remember yours. But I apologize for accidentally touching on a sad topic. Tonight is supposed to be a night of celebration."

"And it will be," I said. "I may not have any close family, but Cara's like a sister to me." I reached for Ronan's hand. "With our upcoming marriage, I look forward to having a family again."

Ronan gave me an encouraging look, before moving forward with our script. "We plan to enjoy a year or two as newlyweds," he said. "But after that, we want children."

"A good plan," Carter said. "It's high time for a new generation of Kingsleys, and I hope that Ava will soon provide you with a son and heir."

In that moment, I grasped what kind of man Ronan's father was and struggled to conceal my distaste. For Carter Kingsley, women were objects. Beneath his charming smile and polished manners, he was an old-school male chauvinist—a selfish man who believed that women existed solely to serve men's needs through sex and producing children, who were in turn expected to toe the line and do as they were told. As I looked at Carter, I felt sad for Ronan, who'd grown up with a stepmother who took every opportunity to put him down and a father who showed little interest in him, beyond demanding that he play the role of obedient son and heir. Maybe my family had never had much money, but at least I'd grown up surrounded by love.

Just then, James returned with a silver tray carrying our drinks. After he served us and left the room, Carter raised his glass.

"To your marriage," he said. "And to the next generation."

As I sipped my Scotch, I glanced at Ronan. His piercing blue gaze was fixed on Carter, and as he raised his glass to his lips, a muscle twitched in his jaw. Although, when it came to his revolving door of women, Ronan had followed in his father's footsteps, Carter's last statement had clearly angered him.

Once again, I asked myself the question that was fast becoming my obsession. How could I reconcile my husband-to-be's history as a Manhattan playboy with moments like this, when his reactions were nothing if not protective?

Who was Ronan Kingsley?

## 19

### RONAN

By the time Veronica reappeared and ordered us to the oceanside room that she and my father used for entertaining, my mood had darkened. Half an hour of watching my father ogle Ava had irritated me, and when he insulted her by implying that her sole purpose in marrying me was to provide the Kingsley family with its next male heir, I barely managed to contain my fury.

Not that my father's behavior was out of character. In the past, when he'd summoned me to attend one or another of Veronica's events, my father had often annoyed me and amused himself by flirting with my dates—but this time was different.

Because Ava was different.

She wasn't anything like the women I usually brought to my father's events, and she deserved better than to be undressed by his gaze, not to mention listening to him talk about her as if she was a brood mare.

As Ava and I worked our way through what felt like an endless series of introductions to Dad and Veronica's guests, my jaw ached with the effort of keeping a smile on my face. But in order to carry off our fake marriage, tonight was only act one of the gauntlet Ava and I needed to run. I couldn't afford to fuck things up by losing my temper.

On the second floor of the house and lined with tall, arched windows overlooking the water, there was a space that had originally been the estate's ballroom and could comfortably hold over two hundred people.

By six thirty, the party was in full swing. Beneath tall, arched windows that overlooked the water, well-dressed Hamptonites filled the oceanside room, which had originally been the estate's ballroom and could comfortably hold over two hundred people. In a corner of the space, a ten-person band played jazz standards, while black-suited servers circulated between clusters of smiling, chattering guests, offering platters of champagne and canapés. Despite this party taking place on short notice, the Southampton elite had turned out in full force to witness the engagement of Carter Kingsley's eldest son.

But it had been nearly twenty years since I'd spent more than an occasional weekend in Southampton, and I avoided my stepmother's Manhattan set as much as possible, which meant that I didn't know many of Dad and Veronica's guests. I'd invited Jack, but he'd had a previous commitment, and Ava's friend Mimi was out of state doing a jewelry show, so she hadn't been able to be here tonight, either.

Which was why when I glimpsed my sister, Cara, heading toward us, I was grateful to see a friendly face. Cara's sleeveless, turquoise-blue dress brought out her bright-blue eyes, and her blond hair shimmered and bounced around her shoulders as she approached.

"Sorry to be late," she said as she embraced Ava and then me. "My Uber driver and I sat on the highway for almost thirty minutes."

"An accident?" Ava asked.

"A fish-truck accident," Cara said, wrinkling her nose. "When we finally got moving again and crawled past the accident site, there were piles of dead fish along the roadside and fish slime all over the road. Fortunately, it didn't appear that anyone was injured—but that stretch of road is never going to smell the same again."

A server approached with a tray of champagne glasses, and Cara seized one. "To your engagement," she said, her eyes twinkling with merriment. "The two of you couldn't look more fabulous together. The perfect Hamptons couple."

I gave my sister a warning look, just as I spotted Portia Hammersley approaching. One of the few Hamptonites who I actually liked, Portia had been friends with our mother. Before her retirement, Portia had run one of Manhattan's most successful art galleries, and despite her age—she had to be at least eighty—she remained vibrant and active. Well-respected in the New York art world, she'd gone out of her way to help Cara with her painting career. But Portia was also one of the sharpest people I knew, and if anyone could suss out that Ava and I weren't truly a couple, Portia would be the one.

I steeled myself and put a smile on my face as the petite, birdlike woman greeted Cara with kisses on both cheeks, before turning to me. Dressed in a winter white gown, with ropes of pearls around her neck, Portia retained the style and manner of the classic beauty that she had been in her youth. I felt bad about lying to her, but it couldn't be helped. Beyond Cara, Jack, and Mimi, I had decided not to broaden the circle of friends who knew the truth about our fake-marriage arrangement. It was simply too risky.

"Well, well," Portia said with an exuberant smile that deepened the network of tiny lines that crisscrossed her face. "The news of your engagement took me by surprise, but now that I see your lovely fiancée, I understand everything."

I introduced Ava, to whom Portia extended a slender, veined hand. "Delighted to meet you," she said to Ava. "I was beginning to fear that Ronan would never meet his match. He's always been a driven young man, and like his father, he works too hard for his own good."

"As Ronan can tell you, I can be a bit of a workaholic myself," Ava said, taking my arm. "But meeting him shifted my priorities. These days, I try to find a balance between spending time with him and taking care of my business, and he does the same for me."

"Ronan and Ava are great together," Cara said with a smile. "I take full credit for introducing them."

"Matchmaking is a risky business," Portia said. "But given the way these two look at each other, I have to congratulate you on your success."

My estimation of Ava's acting ability went up a few more notches, and I relaxed a little. Even Portia had fallen for our act.

"We're very happy together," Ava said. "I feel very fortunate."

"That makes two of us," I said, smiling at my fiancée as our eyes met. I'd never been cut out for marriage, and I might not have gotten lucky in the conventional way, but Ava was playing her role perfectly, and our arrangement was saving me from the toughest spot I'd ever had the misfortune to find myself in. My one regret was that our partnership couldn't extend into the bedroom. For the first time in my life, I was fighting my attraction to a beautiful woman instead of pursuing it.

But that was probably for the best. Like my father, I wasn't the relationship type. Sex was what I had to offer, and Ava had shown no sign of sexual interest in me. Under the circumstances, I was fortunate to have her friendship and loyalty, which was allowing me to save my business.

Which was why, when I spoke, I truly meant what I said.

"I'm the luckiest man on earth."

## 20

AVA

During a lull in the introductions and congratulations that had occupied the first hour of the party, Ronan seized the opportunity to suggest that we slip away so that he could introduce me to the Mortons. Knowing how close Ronan was to Alfred and Evelyn Morton, I had suggested that he might want to tell them the truth about our relationship, but he had refused, saying that while he trusted them completely, given their positions as his father's employees, it would be stressful and unfair to burden them with that knowledge, and the worry for him that would accompany it.

But as we took a flight of stairs down to the first floor, Ronan was silent, and I sensed him steeling himself for what had to be difficult for him.

At the foot of the stairs, we turned right before entering a spacious kitchen, which was completely modern, with state-of-the-art stainless-steel stoves and a bank of matching refrigerators.

"That's Evelyn," Ronan said, gesturing toward a petite, efficient-looking woman in her sixties with attractively cropped gray hair, who stood at the far end of the kitchen, giving instructions to several black-coated servers.

When she spotted us, Evelyn waved, and with a final word to the servers, she hurried over to us. Ronan beamed at her, before sweeping her off her feet in an enthusiastic hug.

"Put me down, you big lug!" she said, laughing. "Introduce me to your fiancée."

When Evelyn referred to me as his fiancée, Ronan paused for a moment, and the fleeting shadow in his eyes told me how hard lying to her was for him. After he put her down, and she regained her footing, she shook my hand with a firm grip. "Delighted to meet you," she said in a crisp British accent. "This one always told me he'd never marry, but he just needed to find the right woman—one who could stand up to him."

"Ava's all that," Ronan said, grinning. "She stands up to me on a daily basis."

"For your own good, I'm sure," Evelyn said. "Ava, you've picked yourself a stubborn man but a good one. Keep that in mind when he gets on your nerves, which he's certain to do on a regular basis."

Ronan looked amused. "Am I really that bad?"

"The baddest of the bad," she said, shooting me a roguish look. "But I love you anyway—and as proof, I've made a batch of your favorite peanut-butter cookies." She stepped to a nearby cupboard, removed a glass cookie jar, and handed it to him.

Ronan beamed at her as he opened the container and held it out to me. "You have to try one. They're addictive."

I took one, tasted it, and had to agree. "Would you consider giving me your recipe?" I asked Evelyn. "I'm not much of a cook, but I enjoy baking."

"I'll copy it out and mail it to you," she said, looking pleased.

"Where's Alfred?" Ronan asked, glancing around as he bit into his cookie. "I want Ava to meet him."

"Upstairs," she said. "Working harder than he should be, after his heart attack last year. But you know Alfred. He refuses to admit that he's no longer a young man."

Ronan's gaze met Evelyn's. "He has standards," they said together, before breaking into laughter.

"It's one of Alfred's lines," Ronan explained. "Whenever anyone suggests anything that might make his life easier, he always says that he has standards."

"That he does," Evelyn said, her hazel eyes twinkling. "But he's also the kindest man on earth, which is why he generally lets me have my way in the end."

A stocky, gray-haired man with blunt features emerged from behind a cluster of caterers. "Plotting against me, love?" he said, winking at me and Ronan. Like his wife, he had a British accent.

"After forty years of marriage, I've no need to plot," she said, giving her husband an affectionate look. "I know you as well as I know myself."

Alfred stepped forward and embraced Ronan, before extending a broad hand to me. "I've been looking forward to meeting you," he said with a smile so genuine that it made his plain, solid face handsome.

I shook his hand. "Likewise. Ronan and Cara have told me so much about you and Evelyn, I feel as if I already know you."

"Where have the years gone?" Alfred said to Evelyn. "It seems only yesterday that our Ronan was a boy, and here he is tonight, engaged to be married."

"I know," she said, looking at Ronan with pride. "It hardly seems possible. But the older I get, the faster time flies."

As I watched Ronan interact with Alfred and Evelyn, I understood him better. With his businesslike manner and quick temper, Ronan held most people at a distance, but beneath that facade, he had a big heart. Growing up with an indifferent father and a hostile stepmother could have made him cold and indifferent, but the man before me, now querying Alfred about his health, was nothing if not warm and caring.

Just then, the young man who had served us whiskey earlier

appeared behind Alfred's right shoulder and spoke to him in a low voice before stepping away.

Alfred looked at Ronan. "You and Ava had best get yourself upstairs," he said. "Mrs. Kingsley's looking for the two of you, and according to James, she's on the warpath."

## 21

### RONAN

After saying our farewells to Alfred and Evelyn, I led Ava out of the kitchen and toward the back staircase, the route that gave us the best chance of dodging Veronica and disappearing back into the party without anyone knowing we had ever left. I didn't want Ava to suffer Veronica's displeasure on my account.

"That was harder than I expected," I whispered to Ava as we entered the stairwell. "Lying to Alfred and Evelyn feels so wrong."

"I feel terrible about it, too," Ava said quietly. "They were so kind and welcoming. Are you sure we can't tell them the truth?"

I shook my head. "I can't dump more stress on them when they're already putting in extra hours due to this party, and then our wedding. Since his heart attack, Alfred's supposed to be taking it easier, but he never does. It's not in his nature."

"What about after the wedding, when things settle down? Couldn't we tell them the truth then?"

"Some secrets are better kept. I don't think I could bear to face their disappointment in me for lying to them—they think I'm better than that. But I can't take the lie back now—what's done is done."

We exited the stairwell, emerged on the second floor, and walked down the hallway that led to the front of the house. As we approached the entrance to the oceanside room and the party, Veronica emerged from the crowd with my half brother, Aiden, who I hadn't seen since Christmas. Aiden was wearing one of the fashion-forward suits that he favored these days, which, to my eye, made him look like a pretty-boy fop. Not that Aiden had given a shit about my opinion since passing his eleventh birthday or so, when he'd sussed out how his mother felt about me and learned to use it to his advantage.

Veronica marched toward us with a grim expression on her face, with Aiden trailing behind her.

"Thanks for nothing," she said in a low voice, her lips tight with anger. "What's your excuse for abandoning your engagement party to slum around the kitchens?"

I met her gaze and, out of consideration for the nearby guests, kept my voice quiet. "You know perfectly well that I always make time to see the Mortons."

"Everyone's aware of your attachment to our butler and house-keeper," Aiden said. "But couldn't you have waited to go downstairs until the party was over? The Andressons wanted to meet you and Ava, and we couldn't find you. You put Mother in an embarrassing position. Your behavior was disrespectful and rude."

"Thank you, Aiden," Veronica said, glaring at me. "Ronan, don't waste your breath with explanations, because there's no excuse for your inconsideration. When are you going to grow up and take your social responsibilities seriously?"

Before I could respond, Ava faced my stepmother, ignoring Aiden altogether. "Now isn't the time for this," she said quietly. "Instead of arguing about responsibilities, we should be seeing to them. Ronan and I are back now, and we'd be delighted to meet the Andressons—or anyone else you'd like us to meet."

Ava's voice was polite but firm, and before Veronica could

respond, Ava turned to me. "Shall we get back to the party and our guests?" she said. "I'd like a glass of champagne."

I held out my arm to her. "Let's go."

She took my arm, and we walked past Veronica and Aiden and toward the oceanside room, where the party appeared just as we'd left it—a cheerful din of voices, music, and clinking glassware, and a crush of well-dressed Hamptonites gossiping and drinking my father's booze. As we entered the room and moved into the crowd, Ava whispered against my ear. "Is Aiden always such a smarmy little ass-kisser?"

"Mostly," I said. "But he's at his worst when his mother's around."

"I suppose she's his audience," Ava said. "He even looks kind of like a male version of her—although he's very handsome."

"As a kid, Aiden wasn't so bad," I said. "Like me at that age, he was obsessed with Star Wars, which used to be a bond between us. But then he grew into a bratty teenager, and since finishing his MBA at Wharton last year, he's been insufferable. Veronica's pampering only inflates his oversized ego."

"Ivy League MBAs tend to emerge from school that way," Ava said. "But over the next few years, exposure to real life should bring your brother down to earth."

"I wouldn't count on it," I said, scanning the crowd for a server. But then I spotted an unwelcome face in the crowd. "Damn it. My stepmother's really outdone herself this time."

"What's she done?"

"She's invited Larissa Storrow—a woman I had a fling with one summer during college. See the tall blonde in the champagne-colored gown? That's her."

"Your college flame's an attractive woman," Ava said. "I like her dress—look, I think she's spotted us. She's coming our way."

After confirming that Ava was right, I turned back to her. Before Larissa reached us, I needed to prepare Ava for what was about to come.

"You need to know that ever since that summer, Larissa despises me and rarely misses an opportunity to humiliate me in public. Veronica knows this, which is why she invited her."

Ava leveled me with a look. "Quickly—give me the gist of what happened between you and Larissa."

Reluctantly, I confessed the embarrassing truth. "A two-week fling when I was nineteen. I moved on—she didn't. I handled it badly; I hurt her feelings—and although I've apologized more than once, she's never forgiven me."

"Don't sweat this," Ava said quietly, tucking her arm into mine. "If she goes there, we'll deal with it together."

Ava meant well, but she'd never seen what Larissa was capable of, and I steeled myself as she approached, with a gleam in her eye that told me everything I dreaded most was about to unfold.

"Hi, Ronan," she said brightly, before turning to Ava. "And you must be the fiancée."

I introduced Ava, who extended her hand to Larissa. "Pleased to meet you," Ava said. "Thank you for celebrating our engagement with us."

"I wouldn't have missed it for anything," Larissa said. She gestured toward the crowd. "As tonight's turnout proves, all of Southampton's curious to meet the woman who's snared one of our most elusive bachelors." She gave Ava a querying look. "Ronan and I were an item at one point—but I suppose you've heard all about that."

"I have," Ava said. "Before we met, Ronan and I both dated other people, so there was romantic history to be shared on both sides."

Larissa leaned toward Ava and lowered her voice. "Romantic is the wrong word for your fiancé's history, I'm afraid. Unless your idea of romance is having a man seduce you, dump you, and then put the moves on your best friend."

As usual, she'd gone straight for my throat. "That was many years ago, and we were both young," I said quietly. "Can't we move beyond the past?"

"I moved beyond it long ago," Larissa said airily. "But I consider it my duty to warn Ava about what she's getting herself into."

"Then consider that duty completed," Ava said coolly. "Like all of us, Ronan made his share of youthful mistakes, but he's been honest with me about those mistakes, and I trust him completely."

Larissa's face flushed, and although she kept her voice low, its tone took on an edge. "Don't be ridiculous. The only person you're fooling is yourself. Ronan Kingsley's the last person on earth anyone should trust."

"Really?" Ava said quietly, staring her down. "Who made you the expert on my fiancé? When was the last time you had an actual conversation with him, instead of trying to make trouble? You're the one who's fooling yourself, Larissa. You say that you've moved on—but you're the one who's stuck in the past, trying to get back at Ronan for something that happened over a decade ago. Grow up, and stop living in the rearview."

"Fine," Larissa snapped. "If you're too stubborn to hear the truth, there's nothing I can do to save you from your own stupidity. One day, he'll betray you—and when that day arrives, I look forward to watching you suffer, just like I did."

And with that, she turned and stalked away.

"Sorry about that," I said. "And thank you. You handled her a hell of a lot better than I've ever managed to do."

"You have nothing to apologize for," Ava said. "That woman needs therapy or something. Seriously. Didn't we all have a messy adolescent romance or two?"

"I had a lot more than that," I said. "It wasn't until my midtwenties that I got better at setting the expectations of the women I dated."

"That's normal," Ava said. "When I look back at my nineteen-year-old self, I cringe too. There was so much I didn't know."

"My stepmother will do anything to make me look bad," I said. "Larissa's just a convenient weapon."

"I know," Ava said. "In a way, I feel bad for her. She seems emotionally unstable, and it was cruel of Veronica to invite her tonight and use her in that way."

"I couldn't agree more," I said. "Once the wedding is behind us, I look forward to avoiding my stepmother for a very long time."

Ava squeezed my arm. "You and me both."

I smiled at Ava, feeling fortunate to have her at my side. In the last half hour, she'd faced not only Veronica but also Larissa and shut them both down. Ava was quick on her feet, she wasn't easily rattled, and she always had my back. I couldn't have had a better partner.

Just then, a server appeared with a tray of champagne. I took two glasses and handed one to Ava.

"Cheers," I said, clinking my glass against hers as I spotted Aiden coming our way. "And drink up, because you're going to need it."

She sipped her champagne. "Any particular reason?"

I lowered my voice. "My bratty brother."

## 22

### AVA

As Aiden approached us, I resolved to give him a second chance. He might be spoiled and egotistical, but he was also a twenty-five-year-old rich kid who'd spent his life cloistered in the kind of exclusive schools that constantly told their students how brilliant they were. And Ronan had said that his half brother was at his worst with Veronica around, which suggested that Aiden might be less unpleasant on his own.

"Mother's thrown you quite the party," Aiden said to us. "I like the band she chose."

"They're excellent," I said. "I especially like the pianist."

Aiden shuffled his feet nervously before looking at Ronan and then at me. "When we met in the hall, I didn't have a chance to congratulate the two of you on your engagement. So...congratulations."

Aiden's discomfort was apparent, but perhaps he was trying to extend some kind of olive branch, so I tried to put him at ease.

"Thank you," I said with a smile. "We're very happy."

"How are the wedding plans going?" Aiden asked.

"Fine," Ronan said coolly, staring his younger brother down in a way that told me he hadn't forgotten Aiden's support of Veronica's criticism of us earlier in the evening.

After several seconds of silence ticked by, I tried to lighten the mood. "Planning a wedding is a big project, and we still have a lot to do. But as Ronan said, it's going fine; Cara and Veronica are helping us work out the details, and everything's falling into place."

"Glad to hear it," Aiden said. "I wouldn't begin to know how to plan a wedding, but then again, I'll never have to." He gave me a humorous look. "If I ever get married, my mother will no doubt insist on planning the entire affair."

"Your mother has a ton of experience throwing events," I said. "It probably feels natural to her to take the lead."

"The Kingsleys are a strong-willed bunch," Aiden said to me. "As you get to know us, you'll find that we all tend to take the lead."

"There's some truth to that," Ronan said.

Was he unbending a little? I hoped so. "I can be kind of the same way," I said. "I suppose that's why I prefer having my own business to working for others."

"Ava's business is doing floral design for events," Ronan said with evident pride. "She started it all on her own, just like I did with Kingsley Tech."

"That's impressive," Aiden said, smiling at me.

"Ava's impressive," Ronan said, reaching for my hand. "I'm a lucky man."

The tension between the brothers seemed to have dissipated—until Aiden spoke again.

"Speaking of Kingsley Tech, rumor on the street is that you're having serious financial problems."

Ronan stiffened beside me, and his grip on my hand tightened. "What you heard is an exaggeration," he said evenly. "Kingsley Tech's expanding and taking on new contracts. But it's nothing I can't handle."

"I hope you're right," Aiden said. "But you should know that the Manhattan rumor mill is betting against you. People are saying that in taking on the Asian contracts, you've significantly overstretched yourself."

"People can say whatever the hell they like," Ronan said curtly. "They're wrong."

"For your own sake, I hope you know what you're doing," Aiden said.

"Of course I do," Ronan growled. "Who do you think I am?"

Aiden held up his hands. "No offense, OK? Based on what I heard, I was concerned."

Had he accepted Ronan's explanation? I wasn't sure. Aiden might be young and inexperienced, but he was also a Wharton-educated MBA, and the rumors that he'd heard were dangerously close to the truth.

Sensing Ronan's annoyance and hoping to shift the conversation onto safer ground, I smiled at Aiden. "I know you work at Kingsley Capital with Carter, but what does your job entail? What kind of work do you do?"

An expression of pride took over Aiden's lean, handsome face. "Over the past few months, I've moved into forex stuff. Dad's put me in charge of a team that's developing a new line of hedge funds."

"I know what a hedge fund is," I said. "But what does 'forex' mean?"

"It's slang for foreign exchange," Aiden said. "I've decided to specialize in working with foreign currencies."

"Why would you want to do that?" Ronan asked.

Aiden looked defensive. "It's interesting work."

"Maybe to you," Ronan said. "To each their own, I suppose—but I can't think of anything duller than staring at currency numbers all day."

Aiden's expression shifted, and he leaned toward Ronan. "I came over here to make an effort to have a decent conversation with my brother, and all I get is attitude? Fuck you. Mother always says that trying to get along with you is pointless, and you know what? Maybe she's right."

And with that, he walked away.

I hadn't been fortunate enough to have siblings, and I couldn't stand to watch Ronan throwing away any chance of a positive relationship with his brother. Aiden might be a brat, but he also clearly craved his older brother's approval, which meant there was still hope that they could form a connection.

If only Ronan was willing to be the mature older brother I knew he could be. If he was willing to step up and be the bigger person.

I looked at Ronan, who was calmly sipping his champagne. "Is there anywhere nearby that we can have a few minutes of privacy?"

"We can step into the sitting room across the hall," he said. "What's this about?"

"I'll tell you as soon as we're alone."

When we reached the sitting room, I closed the door behind us, crossed the room to the single arched window, and looked out over the ocean before turning to face him. "Why did you have to be so hard on your brother just now?"

He looked surprised. "Why the hell would I waste energy being nice to Aiden? He's a worthless little shit. I may have finished what just went down, but Aiden started it. The only reason he bothered to talk to us was to deliver that poison pill of malicious gossip. What I said to him was no more than he deserved."

"I disagree. He's young and socially awkward, but I don't think he meant badly. There's a part of him that wants your attention and approval."

"I don't care what he wants," Ronan said, his voice rising. "As long as he remains his mother's goddamned pawn, he's getting nothing from me."

"Have you even considered trying to separate your relationship with Aiden from your relationship with your stepmother? If you gave Aiden a break and stopped assuming the worst of him, maybe the two of you could build a better relationship."

Ronan stepped closer to me, so close that I could feel the heat radiating from his powerful body. "You don't know what the hell you're talking about. Veronica destroyed any possibility of me and Aiden getting along years ago."

"I may not know everything about your family, but you shouldn't forget that Aiden's just beginning his adult life. He's at the stage when people become more independent and start thinking for themselves."

Ronan snorted dismissively. "Aiden? Thinking for himself? That'll be the day."

"If that's your attitude, then you might as well forget about having a brother."

He glared at me. "Believe me, I already have."

Just then, I noticed that the door that I had closed to give us privacy was now open. Who had opened it—or had I not closed it securely? In the doorway, Veronica stood, with a curious expression on her face. Had she heard our raised voices? And if so, how much had she heard?

Ronan stood just in front of me with his back to his stepmother, and his face was flushed with anger. No doubt my face betrayed my emotion as well. If Veronica came in and saw us like this, what would she think? Would her suspicions about our relationship rise to new heights? And if they did, what would that mean for our fake-marriage arrangement?

Desperate to salvage the situation, I did the only thing I could think of.

"Veronica's behind you," I said in a low voice. "Kiss me now."

## 23

RONAN

When Ava told me to kiss her, I couldn't have been more surprised. But despite the argument we'd just been having, I trusted her judgment that kissing her was what was necessary to maintain the illusion of our relationship. It didn't hurt that I'd been fantasizing about getting my hands on her all night, ever since she'd stepped out of her room looking sexy as hell, and my body had responded in ways that reminded me of my teenage years.

I stepped forward, pinned her shoulders against the frame of the window behind her, and kissed her with everything in me. I might never get another chance to do this, and I intended to make the most of the opportunity.

When my mouth touched down on hers, electricity crackled between us. Her lips parted beneath mine, and the little moan that escaped her brought my cock to full attention. I kissed her slowly, deeply, letting my tongue trace leisurely circles around hers, before moving my hands to cup her breasts, tracing their contours before seeking out her hardened nipples, which I flicked lightly with my thumbs.

She gasped in pleasure, and her hands reached for me, exploring my chest and traveling downward before gripping my hips and tugging me closer, as my erection hardened against her body.

The moment I'd caught Ava checking me out flashed through my mind. What did this kiss mean? Was she hot for me, too? Had we both been fighting attraction to each other?

As her body molded against mine, I drank in her delicate, floral scent and tasted the subtle tang of champagne in her mouth. Her tongue thrust against mine, sparring in a heated, sensual dance that inflamed my lust for her and erased any remaining doubt. Regardless of our arrangement, regardless of what had prompted Ava to ask for this kiss, she was every bit as into it as I was.

A door closed, heels clicked, and my stepmother's voice spoke behind me.

"Spare me," she said. "What will you two get up to next? First hiding in the kitchens and now rutting like teenagers?" Reluctantly, I released Ava, and we both turned toward Veronica's scowling face.

"I apologize," Ava said, shooting me a look that told me she had this. "The two of us got carried away, which I hope you can understand. We didn't intend any disrespect—surely you remember what it's like to be in love and to find your lover irresistible."

Veronica's lips tightened. "This is an engagement party, not a bordello. Is it really too much to ask that you act your age for a few hours? Or, if that proves impossible, at least have the decency to lock yourselves in a bathroom? There are only fourteen to choose from."

As my stepmother continued her rant, I pretended to listen while watching Ava out of the corner of my eye. Flushed with arousal and embarrassment, she was hotter than ever, and two thoughts formed in my mind.

The first was wonderment that I had managed to keep my hands off her since she'd moved in with me.

The second was that I no longer had any intention of doing so.

After the party ended, the drive back to Manhattan seemed endless, and from the expression on Ava's face, I knew that she wanted to talk about what had happened earlier—the kiss that had unraveled any pretense that we didn't want to fuck each other's brains out.

That pretense was dead.

But during the party's final hour, we hadn't had an opportunity to speak in private, and we couldn't risk an open conversation in front of my father's driver. So, throughout the ride home, I stared out the window, watching the night-darkened landscape flash by, while Ava did the same at the window opposite mine.

When we finally reached my building, it was just after eleven. Under the glow of the streetlights, I helped Ava out of the car and walked her inside. During the elevator ride to my floor, our eyes met. What I saw in her gaze was a desire equal to my own, but knowing Ava, she'd probably try to talk us both out of it. She'd insist that given our fake-marriage arrangement, having sex wasn't a good idea.

But that conversation wasn't on my agenda.

What was on my agenda was a new arrangement. One that recognized the sizzling chemistry between us. One that acknowledged our attraction and allowed us to enjoy it. Our life together might not be what either of us would have chosen, but it didn't have to be sexless. Not if I could persuade Ava to see things as they actually were. Until tonight's kiss, I'd held myself back because sex was all I had to offer, and nothing in her behavior had hinted at any attraction to me. But tonight's kiss had changed everything, revealing a chemistry that was off the charts.

As soon as the apartment door closed behind us, Ava faced me. "We need to talk."

"We do, and we will," I said. "But first, we need to do this."

And with that, I swept her into my arms and kissed her with all the heat that was pent up inside me. Her lips parted, and her body melted against mine, surrendering to me in ways that reaffirmed everything I already knew. She wanted this every bit as much as I did—she just wasn't quite as ready to admit it.

Fortunately, I was the man to take her there. It was one thing to say no to possibility, but after I fucked her the way I intended to, she'd have to say no to reality—which wouldn't be so easy. Not after I rocked her world the way I knew I could.

"We shouldn't," she gasped when we came up for air. "Not that I don't want to—you know I do—but it's a bad idea."

I kissed her again, before lifting her in my arms and carrying her toward the bedroom. The couch was closer, but for what I had in mind, we needed my king-sized bed.

"This isn't a good idea," she said as she raised her head to kiss me again.

"No," I said. "This is the best idea either of us has had since you moved in."

# 24

## AVA

In a haze of desire, Ronan and I kissed our way to the master suite, where he turned the lights to a low setting, before resting me on my feet and smoothly unzipping my dress, which fell to my feet in a shimmering pile of red fabric, leaving me standing in my lacy black underthings and four-inch heels.

"Fuck, Ava," he said as his heated gaze swept over my body, consuming me with its single-minded intensity, before he took me in his arms and kissed me within an inch of my life. His strong hands roved over my body, teasing and exploring, and when he delved a hand into my panties and ran a finger over my swollen folds, I shuddered with arousal, wet with need for him and what we were about to do.

He raised his hand to his lips, licked the taste of me off his finger, and looked into my eyes. "You taste like heaven, Ava. Even sweeter than I'd imagined. I can't wait to sink my mouth between your legs."

I'd never wanted anything as badly as I wanted him right now, and as my last shred of resistance evaporated into lust-fueled oblivion, we quickly shed the remainder of our clothing. Nothing existed but the two of us and our overwhelming need to satisfy our desire for each other.

Naked, we fell onto the bed together and kissed deeply. When we came up for air, Ronan pulled back and gave me a scorching look, before nibbling his way down my torso, dipping his dark head between my thighs and tracing my throbbing sex with his tongue.

I released a little moan, my breath coming in gasps, as my universe went electric. Under Ronan's mouth, every nerve in my body was on fire, every inch of my body charged with need. As his tongue alternated between long, lazy strokes and delicate, teasing flicks against my clit, waves of arousal built within me, rising toward orgasm with the inevitability of an approaching tsunami.

When my release washed over me, its force shattered me. Pleasure ripped through my body, and I cried out as whiteness filled my vision, blinding me. At twenty-seven, I was hardly new to sex, but I'd never come so hard in my life. I hadn't known it was possible.

"Oh my God," I said, clutching Ronan's shoulders against my still-trembling body. "That was amazing. You're amazing."

"You haven't seen anything yet," he said, with a hint of satisfaction in his deep voice. "That was just an appetizer."

He kissed me, and when I tasted myself on his lips, a fresh hunger ignited within me. I wanted to touch him, to taste him, to explore every flavor of his body as he had mine.

But Ronan had other ideas. He moved to my side, and I heard the sound of a foil packet tearing. When he turned back to me, his thick erection was encased in a condom.

"Ready for the next course?" he said, quirking an eyebrow at me.

I ran my hand over his broad chest, exploring his defined muscles. "Mmmm. I can't wait."

"That makes two of us," he said. "I've been fantasizing about this for days."

I wrapped my arm around his waist. "Really?"

"I've done a lot of thinking about exactly what I want to do to you," he said with a mischievous grin. "It's been keeping me up at night."

I laughed. "Seriously?"

"Seriously," he said. "But tonight, that kiss made me realize we both wanted the same thing."

I ran my fingers through his thick, dark hair. "So here we are—keeping you up at night again."

"Sleep can wait," he said, dipping his head to bite my left nipple and then my right, before brushing his cock against my folds, teasing my sensitive, dampened flesh with its tip. Then his fingers filled me, sliding in and out, as he circled my clit with his thumb, reigniting my desire.

Shivering with want, I met his intense blue gaze, now darkened by a lust equal to my own. "I need you now. I need you inside me."

I was so wet, so ready, that when he slid into me, I nearly came again. For a long moment, he didn't move—he just looked at me, with an unmistakable hunger that erased any lingering doubts about my desirability to him. He wanted me as badly as I wanted him.

But when Ronan began to move, there was nothing tentative about it. He was as commanding, as masterful with my body as he was with everything else in his life. With slow, deliberate thrusts, he drove waves of sensation through me, and I joined his rhythm with thrusts of my own, my blood thrumming in my ears and my skin tingling, supercharged, as my arousal built.

When his thrusts quickened, I was already close. My world shrank to a pinpoint and then exploded as fireworks of sensation laced through me. My body bowed against his as we came together, screaming our pleasure into the dimly lit bedroom.

My heart pounding in my ears, I collapsed back onto the bed and released a sigh as my world slowly tilted back into focus.

Ronan turned away briefly to dispose of his condom, before stretching out beside me and reaching for my hand.

It was the first time I'd taken a long look at him unclothed, but I hadn't guessed wrong about the body beneath his expensive suits. His shoulders were broad, his arms corded with thick muscle. His powerful chest was dusted with dark hair that trailed down to firm six-pack abs. His torso tapered into narrow hips and long, beautifully muscled thighs. His cock, now at half-mast, was thick and as beautifully formed as the rest of him.

And his ass? If I'd been the poetry-writing type—which I wasn't—I could have written a poem on that subject. Many guys just worked on their upper bodies, but Ronan clearly wasn't one of those guys. He had the kind of tight, rounded butt that was worthy of a porn calendar.

"You have the most gorgeous ass," I said, running my hand over it appreciatively.

He gazed into my eyes. "And you've been hiding a banging body behind the loose blouses and jeans you usually wear."

"Work clothes aren't supposed to be sexy," I said. "Although I've always had a weakness for a man in a well-fitted suit."

He gave me a humorous look. "Want me to put mine back on? I will, if you ask nicely, and offer up an appropriate bribe."

I laughed. "As it turns out, I like you naked even better—although I'm still not sure it's wise for us to be doing this. As much as I enjoyed being with you just now, it's way outside our arrangement."

"Let's table that discussion until tomorrow morning," he said. "Right now, I'd much rather make love to you again."

And when I smiled my agreement, he did.

## 25

### AVA

When I awoke the next morning in Ronan's king-sized bed, it took me several seconds to remember where I was—and how I had ended up there. After having our way with each other deep into the night, we had finally collapsed in a tangle of twisted sheets and intertwined limbs and drifted into sleep together.

Careful not to wake him, I disentangled myself from him, got up, and returned to my bedroom, where I made a beeline for the shower in the adjoining bathroom. My head felt fuzzy, muddled by sleep and sex, and I needed to wake the hell up.

I'd had sex with my fake husband-to-be, and it had been earth shattering. Mind blowing. And when he woke up, I had a feeling he'd want to do it all over again.

Hell, I wanted to do it all over again.

What should I do? Or not do?

I didn't even begin to know—but hopefully, a shower and a vat of coffee would kick my brain into gear. It had to, because before I faced

Ronan, I had some serious thinking to do—and I didn't have much time before he woke up.

As I lathered and rinsed my body beneath the shower's hot spray, moments from last night flashed through my mind. Our unexpected kiss and the pent-up desire it had unleashed. Ronan's eyes, veiled with lust, gazing into mine. My body arching against his as I screamed my release. The memory of his strong hands on my skin and the pleasant ache that still reverberated throughout my body.

I'd had a boyfriend in college and a fiancé in my midtwenties, and I'd enjoyed an active sex life with each of them. But what I'd experienced last night was on a whole different level.

Until last night, I hadn't had sex for two years. Could I explain my desire for Ronan—and my body's response to his touch—as sheer sexual deprivation?

As I turned the shower off, stepped out, and began drying myself, I knew that I couldn't. I'd gone even longer between breaking up with my college boyfriend and getting together with my ex-fiancé Brian, and while Brian and I had fucked like bunnies when we first started sleeping together, it had never been like last night.

Over the past weeks, Ronan and I had become friends, and at this point, what attracted me to him went far beyond his looks. His intelligence, his thoughtfulness, his ability to make me laugh—in so many ways, he was a man I could seriously fall for.

And there was my dilemma.

Should I turn my back on the hottest sex of my life in an attempt to put the brakes on my deepening feelings for Ronan—or should I risk heartbreak and allow myself to do what every cell in my body craved? Beyond that, would sleeping together strengthen our fake-marriage arrangement or create conflicts that I didn't know how to anticipate?

As I put on jeans, a T-shirt, and a lightweight sweater, I felt certain of what Ronan would say. He'd tell me how much he wanted me and insist that sleeping together wouldn't affect our arrangement in any negative way.

It wasn't difficult to imagine what my two closest friends would say, either. Mimi would tell me to go for it. She'd say that if our relationship began to feel too unbalanced, that I could always end the sex and revert to the original fake-marriage arrangement. She'd say that as long as Ronan and I were open and honest with each other, that everything would work out just fine.

Cara's attitude would be different. She'd be torn between warning me that her brother was a confirmed man-whore and hoping against hope that he and I would fall in love.

Not that there was any danger of that happening—at least not on Ronan's side. He'd been with hundreds of women and hadn't fallen in love with any of them. His life had a pattern, and there was no reason to expect him to change.

But my life had a pattern too. For me, sex had always been deeply intertwined with love, and ultimately, I hoped to find a man who wanted the same things that I did—lifelong commitment and creating a family together.

On the other hand, no matter what I decided, finding love wasn't in the cards for me anytime in the next two years. I'd signed an agreement, and I meant to keep it. Since finding Mr. Right wasn't an option, what would be the harm in continuing to have sex with Ronan—or at least allowing myself a few more nights of pleasure before calling it off?

Was I fooling myself? Could I break my own pattern and have a friends-with-benefits relationship, without falling head-over-heels in love? Could I enjoy our sizzling sexual chemistry without craving more? Could I maintain enough emotional distance from Ronan to safeguard my heart?

And then I stopped myself. I was a strong, smart woman, and my eyes were wide open. Ronan was never going to fall in love with me, but I didn't have to let myself fall in love with him, either. Instead of fighting reality, I could choose to accept it, set a few reasonable boundaries, and enjoy our electric sexual connection for what it was.

Which was exactly what I planned to do.

## 26

### RONAN

When I woke up, Ava was gone. As I got up and headed for the shower, a sense of disappointment hung over me. Despite how great last night had been for both of us, she'd probably shut things down between us because of the goddamned marriage arrangement.

The arrangement I still needed to save my ass.

But as I went through my morning rituals, my mood rebounded. Although Ava's temperament was more cautious than my own, she was also a woman who went after what she wanted. And last night had made it clear that she wanted me.

We just needed to negotiate a new arrangement—one that included sex.

And I intended to win that negotiation.

As I put on a T-shirt and jeans, I focused on my strategy. I would listen to Ava, figure out what she wanted, and propose a new arrangement that satisfied both of our needs.

With that in mind, I headed for the kitchen and a cup of the coffee that Ava had no doubt made already, since she'd awakened before me.

When I reached the kitchen, Ava was sitting on the couch in the living area, sipping coffee, and watching the morning news.

"Good morning," I called as I reached for the coffee pot. "How did you sleep?"

"Like a rock," she said. "But once you've had your coffee and woken up, we need to talk."

I poured myself a cup of coffee, added a splash of half-and-half, headed for the living room, and sat down in my armchair.

"Talk to me," I said. "But before you begin, there's one thing I need to say."

She reached for the remote and turned off the television. "What's that?"

"Thank you for last night. You're an amazing lover, and I need to be straight with you. All I've thought about since waking up is how much I want to make love to you again."

She gave me a tentative half smile. "You're the one who's amazing, and I'd be lying if I said that I didn't want to have sex with you again. But it isn't that simple. We have to consider our agreement, because it ties us together for the next two years—and there's too much at stake to fuck it up with...well, fucking."

"Agreed," I said. "What would you propose?"

She met my gaze. "A few ground rules. They don't have to become part of our written agreement—but if we're going to do this friends-with-benefits thing, we need to make sure we're on the same page."

Relief washed through me. Ava's focus on setting rules confirmed that she was already leaning my way. All I needed to do now was avoid screwing up.

"What rules would you suggest?" I asked.

She shifted her position on the couch but didn't speak, and I sensed her unease. "You seem nervous," I said. "If there's something you want to say, just say it."

"It's just that this kind of relationship is new to me," she said.

"It's new to me too."

"I suppose I'm still trying to figure it out."

I gave her a relaxed smile. "Don't sweat it—we'll figure this out together."

When she opened her mouth, I understood her hesitation. "Safety, for one. I'm on birth control, and I know I'm clean, but—"

To spare her the stress of searching for a polite way to ask *that* question, I cut her off. "No worries on that count—I've always been a safe-sex kind of guy."

"When was your last test?"

"When I had my annual checkup last month. You're the only person I've been with since then. If you'd like to see my results, I don't mind showing them to you."

"That won't be necessary," she said. "I trust your word—but we still need to discuss a few more issues."

"Tell me what's on your mind."

"I'd like to maintain separate bedrooms and continue sleeping in my own bed."

"Not an issue," I said. "Sleep wherever you're most comfortable."

"I'm just trying to be clear," Ava said. "If this is going to work, we need to be on the same page about what we expect from each other."

"That makes sense," I agreed.

"If we're going to add sex to our arrangement, it needs to be a one-day-at-a-time thing," she said. "If either of us wants to stop that aspect of our relationship, or take time off from it, all we should have to do is say so."

"That's fair," I said. After last night, she wouldn't want to stop anytime soon. If she changed her mind down the road, I'd face that when it happened. "Anything else?"

"Just that we really can't afford to let our sexual relationship interfere with our marriage arrangement. There's too much on the line."

"Agreed," I said. Based on everything Ava had already told me, I had a decent sense of what she needed to hear from me, so I did my best to reassure her. "Our marriage arrangement is business, and nothing about the agreement we signed needs to change. Just think of sex as a bonus. Anytime you don't feel like being with me, all you have to do is say so. I'll always respect your wishes, and if you want to stop having sex at some point in the future, that decision won't change the rest of our relationship."

I didn't have any issue with saying those words, because I meant them. In my own way, I was a gentleman. Unlike some guys I knew, on the rare occasions that a woman gave me a firm no, I didn't push back. I just moved on to a more receptive audience.

Ava's lips quirked. "A bonus. That's a hell of a description for what we did last night."

I raised an eyebrow at her. "There's more where that came from."

"I'm well aware of that—and you're a good salesman."

Since the mood seemed to be lightening, I gave her a suggestive look. "Should I take that to mean you're sold?"

Her voice turned teasing. "Let's say I'm considering your offer. But before we close the deal, I'd like a full list of features and benefits."

"Let's see," I said, playing along. "I'm offering honesty, a decent sense of humor, freedom from expectations—and a big cock."

"Nice features," she said. "What about the benefits?"

"Unless what I'm remembering was a truly mind-blowing dream, we both experienced the benefits last night."

She gave me a wry look. "You could say that again."

I grinned at her. "Want another test drive before you make up your mind? Because if you do, I'm ready to go."

## 27

### AVA

Over the next few weeks, my life was a nonstop flurry of activity. Between planning our wedding and running our respective businesses, Ronan and I were on the go virtually nonstop.

But despite our busy schedule, we found time for sex.

Lots of sex.

And in between having our way with each other, we talked—sometimes deep into the night. Mostly, we chatted about day-to-day things, but gradually, Ronan opened up to me. And as he did, I understood him better.

One night, when we were stretched out on his bed, relaxed and replete from the orgasm we'd just shared, he spoke of his mother.

"I wish you could have known her," he said, spooning his body behind me and wrapping a strong arm around me. "She was the opposite of my stepmother—gentle, soft-spoken, and kind. Everyone adored her—including me. When I was five or six years old, I used to pick flowers from the estate's gardens and bring them to her."

"I remember doing something similar when I was a kid," I said. "Since we lived next door to a farm, I used to pick wildflowers for my mother in the fields. Maybe that's when my interest in arranging flowers began."

"I don't remember bothering to arrange the flowers I picked," Ronan said. "But one of the great things about my mother was that when I handed her some lopsided bouquet or half-assed drawing, she always acted as if I'd given her the best gift in the world."

I reached for his hand and squeezed it, remembering my own mother. "My mother was the same way. She understood that scribbly drawings and fistfuls of flowers are offerings of love."

"What about your father?" Ronan asked. "What was he like?"

"His work as an engineer kept him on the road a lot," I said. "But he called my mother and me every night, and when he was at home, he went out of his way to plan special outings with us—like a trip to the beach or the zoo. My favorite was playing minigolf at one of the parks near where we lived. I suck at most sports, but I love badminton and minigolf."

"Sounds like your parents got along well," he said.

"As far as I know, they did. They were affectionate with each other, and I don't remember them arguing."

"Mine didn't argue either," he said. "At least not in front of me. But Mom often seemed sad, and a few times, I saw her crying. It wasn't until years after her death, when I caught Dad cheating on Veronica, that I began to understand my mother's unhappiness."

In that moment, I began to grasp the paradox that was Ronan Kingsley. The mystery of why a thoughtful, caring man had chosen the life of a Manhattan playboy.

As a child, he'd witnessed his mother's pain due to his father's infidelity and then watched his father treat his stepmother the same way. After that experience, it wasn't surprising that as a man, he'd avoided relationships and the commitments that went with them. Maybe he didn't believe in love—or maybe he feared hurting someone the way his father had hurt his mother.

As the rhythm of Ronan's breathing shifted, telling me that he was drifting toward sleep, I lay awake, imagining the five- or six-year-old boy who he would have been when he began to grapple with the rift in his parents' marriage and considering how traumatic his exposure to his mother's suffering must have been for him.

Was everyone broken in some way? Did we all carry scars that made us wary of love, fearful of the pain it could bring?

In the aftermath of discovering my ex-fiancé's betrayal and breaking off my engagement, I'd seen a therapist for several months, a wise and kind woman who had helped me see my own scars. For months before the breakup, there had been warning signs that Brian was cheating on me, but due to the strength of my desire for commitment and family—a desire that my therapist connected to the loss of my own family—I'd overlooked and dismissed those signs. I'd explained them away.

I'd wanted to believe in Brian, so I'd fooled myself—until reality smacked me in the face.

In my relationship with Ronan, I'd managed to deviate from my old pattern—at least to some degree. Unlike with my ex-fiancé, I wasn't expecting Ronan to fulfill my dreams of home and family. I knew better than to indulge in that fantasy. Still, no amount of self-discipline could keep me from wishing that he returned my feelings.

Patterns were tough to break—and I had to admit that I hadn't fully broken mine.

But by coming home to me every night, Ronan was breaking his pattern too. Beyond that, he was starting to share parts of his past, revealing more of himself to me. Our intimacy didn't feel one-sided.

Was our growing closeness as mutual as it felt, or was I fooling myself as I had with my ex? Was I projecting my own desires onto Ronan?

Or was our fake relationship slowly becoming real?

## 28

### RONAN

"I just got back from the fitting for my best-man monkey suit," Jack said. "It's hard to believe, but in two weeks, you'll be a married man."

I leaned back in my office chair, closed the laptop on my desk, and regarded my business partner as he shut the door of my office behind him, crossed the room, and settled his tall frame into the chair across from me.

"It was hard for me to believe it myself at first," I said. "But at this point, I'm used to the idea. It feels good to know that we'll soon be able to put our financial troubles behind us. After the wedding, the lawyers will need a few days to do their thing, but once the paperwork goes through, I'll have full access to my trust money."

Jack gave me a mischievous look. "It can't hurt that Ava agreed to sweeten the deal."

I grinned at him. "Trust me, I'm feeling no pain."

"Lucky dog," Jack said, shaking his head. "How the hell did you manage to find a fake wife who not only checks all the boxes but also signs on for the porn movie you call your life? She's even got that sparkle in her eye—the look of a woman who knows how to give a guy the ride of a lifetime."

"Get your dirty mind off my fiancée," I said mildly. "She's mine."

He eyed me, and his expression turned thoughtful. "Ava's different, isn't she?"

"Of course she's different. For one thing, she's a Harvard grad and an entrepreneur, not a party girl. For another, she and I have a business agreement—the one you helped me write."

"Maybe," Jack said. "Or maybe you really like her."

"I do like her—just not in the way you mean. You know I don't do relationships."

"You never have. But there's a first time for everything."

"You know I'm not that kind of guy," I said. "Women like Ava and my sister deserve better than the likes of you and me. I can't imagine limiting myself to one woman for the rest of my life."

"That makes two of us," Jack said. "Although my older brother is proof that meeting the right woman can change a guy's thinking. Ever since Marc met Julia, he hasn't so much as looked at another woman."

"Maybe that can happen for some," I said. "But I'm too much like my old man. I'm just grateful that Ava and I are getting along well and that our fake-marriage arrangement is working out better than I could have imagined. Fortunately, she's a better actor than I am. She's saved my ass with Veronica more than a few times."

"How's your stepmother these days?" Jack asked.

I shrugged. "Bitchy. Annoying. Difficult. In other words, her usual self. But Ava's great at handling her. Whenever Veronica tries to stick a knife in her, Ava dodges it like a pro."

"So things are going smoothly," Jack said.

"As smoothly as they can, given that between wedding stuff and work, the past few weeks have been crazy. But that's winding down, and I'm nearly caught up on work. Today's Friday, and if nothing blows up between now and the end of the day, I'm hoping to take the weekend off."

"It's the next-to-last weekend before your wedding," Jack said. "As your business partner, I'm ordering you to take it off. If there's anything that can't wait until Monday, dump it on my desk. I'll deal with it."

"Thanks," I said. "I appreciate that. Unless Ava has other plans, I'd like to take her out to do something fun tomorrow. She's had to put up with my stepmother throughout the wedding arrangements, and I want to do something to thank her, but I haven't managed to come up with any good ideas."

Jack raised an eyebrow at me. "It's called a date, bro. You're talking about taking Ava on a date."

"Call it whatever you like. I just want to do something nice for her."

"What's Ava into? What kind of things does she enjoy?"

"Movies. Art. Flowers. Good food and wine."

"You could take her out for dinner and a movie," Jack said. "Or the two of you could hit the Metropolitan Museum of Art. That place is so huge, there's something for everyone. As for flowers, now that spring's here, you could always include a walk through Central Park in your plans."

When Jack mentioned the park, an idea struck me. "Ava likes minigolf. Isn't there a minigolf course in Hudson River Park?"

Surprise flashed across Jack's face. "There is. I think it's at Pier Twenty-Five."

I opened my laptop, Googled Pier 25, and skimmed the information on my screen. "The course looks well-maintained, and it just opened for the season. There's also a nearby restaurant that looks pretty good. We can go for a stroll, play minigolf, and then have dinner."

"What's the name of the restaurant?"

"City Vineyard."

"I've been there," Jack said. "It's a nice place, with good food and a great view of the river." He gave me a thumbs-up. "Sounds like you've got this under control."

"Thanks for the ideas," I said. "I think I have."

# 29

## RONAN

Fortunately for my Saturday afternoon outing with Ava, the day turned out to be gorgeous. As we strolled hand in hand down one of the sidewalks that led through Hudson River Park, a broad strip of greenery that ran along the Hudson River, the sun felt pleasantly warm on my skin, and a breeze from the river ruffled my hair.

We were far from the only New Yorkers taking advantage of the fine weather. As we moved through the park, we passed joggers, young parents pushing strollers, and couples of all ages. The shouts of children rang out from play areas, and when we passed the park's large skate park, a dozen teenagers on skateboards zipped around its ramps, polishing and perfecting their stunts.

When we reached Pier 25, a long pier that stretched far into the Hudson River, Ava glanced at the playground to our left and then at the boat-charter business to our right.

"I've never been here," she said. "Is your mysterious surprise going out on a boat?"

"No," I said. "It's still chilly on the water at this time of year. But we'll definitely go for a sail this summer."

We turned left, walked past the playground, and as we approached the minigolf course, I watched Ava closely, anticipating the moment when she realized what it was. When an angular kiosk with a large GOLF sign came into view, her face lit up.

"This has to be it," she said.

I smiled at her. "It is."

As we approached the course and glimpsed the first few greens, she turned to me with a visible excitement that confirmed I'd made the right choice.

"This course is totally different," she said. "I've never seen anything like it. Most minigolf courses are all about windmills and waterfalls, but this looks like an actual golf course, only much smaller."

"I see hills, rocks, and sand traps," I said. "But overall, the course designers seem to have gone for a park-like look. Want to play a round?"

"You know I do," she said, wrapping an arm around my waist. "Thank you for thinking of this and bringing me here."

"My pleasure," I said and stepped up to the kiosk to pay the attendant.

After I paid and received our golf balls and putters, I handed one of each to Ava, and we headed toward the first hole. When we reached it, a family of four occupied the green, and while we waited for them to finish, a thought occurred to me.

I turned to Ava. "What would you like to bet on the outcome of our game?"

"Loser buys dinner?" she suggested.

"Come on. We can do better than that."

She gave me a mischievous look, before leaning against me and whispering in my ear. "Winner chooses what we do first when we get home tonight."

"That's more like it," I said in a low voice. "But let's raise the stakes. Winner ties loser to the bed—and has his way with her."

She made a face at me. "You mean *her* way with him. Because this is one game I'm actually good at, and I'm going to whip your ass."

I didn't believe that for a minute. I'd played golf since I was a kid, and while I was no Tiger Woods, I was pretty good—not to mention motivated. As I imagined tying Ava to my bed, my cock twitched in response.

"Really?" I said. "You're that good?"

"Consider yourself warned. Now, are you prepared to put your freedom on the line—or are you going to chicken out on me?"

I grinned at her. "Me, chicken out? Never."

The foursome ahead of us moved on to the next hole, and Ava gestured toward the green. "Go ahead. Let's see what you've got."

"Ladies first," I said. "Take your time."

She positioned her golf ball on the tee-off pad, before standing to its left and gripping her putter far too rigidly.

"You're holding your club the wrong way," I said. "And you need to loosen up your hips."

She gave me a don't-mess-with-my-mojo look. "This is what works for me."

With an awkward, tentative swing that would have made a golf pro cringe, she hit the ball, which trickled across the green and stopped several inches from the hole.

"Nice one," I said appreciatively.

"I'm out of practice," she said as she walked up to the ball and tapped it into the hole. "I should have made that shot."

My first putt overshot the hole, but my second went in. "I'm just getting warmed up," I said, stretching my arms and twisting my hips from side to side.

"So am I," she said, throwing me a confident smile. "Prepare to lose, Kingsley—because you're going down."

"You're the one who's going down, Walker." I leaned close to her as we strolled toward the second hole and lowered my voice. "Down on my bed, with your hands and feet tied to the frame."

Ava laughed as she dropped her ball on the tee-off pad of the second hole. "We'll see about that."

By the time we finished playing the front nine, I was less sure of the outcome. As weird-looking as Ava's putting technique was, it worked for her, and my score was only one stroke under hers. And at the eleventh hole, which featured a hill that funneled the ball down into a hole that dumped it out near the real hole, I screwed up badly enough for Ava to seize the lead, which she held until the fifteenth hole, when her ball missed a narrow bridge and plopped into the water beneath.

When we reached the eighteenth and final hole, we were tied—and then, Ava pulled off a hole-in-one. As the ball rolled into the hole, she shot me a bright, victorious look but said nothing as I positioned my ball on the tee-off pad, eyed the hole, and prepared to swing.

I hit the ball and watched it roll toward the hole, willing it to go in. If it didn't, I would be getting tied to my own bed, a prospect with which I wasn't entirely comfortable. I'd never let a woman tie me up before, and when I'd proposed the bet with Ava, it had never occurred to me that she might actually win.

As the ball approached the hole, it slowed but not quite enough, and instead of dropping into the hole, it clinked against its rim and spun away from it, stopping several inches away.

*Fuck.* "Congratulations," I said, forcing a smile I didn't feel. "You win."

"I got lucky," she said. "I almost never get a hole-in-one, and we're so evenly matched, the game could totally have gone either way."

"No need for modesty," I said, resolving to take my loss like a man. "You played a great game, and you won, fair and square."

She stepped toward me, linked her arm through mine, and we exited the course together.

"You're a good sport," she said. "And now that I've won, there's something I need to confess."

"What's that?"

She gave me a teasing look. "I'm really looking forward to claiming my prize."

## 30

### AVA

After leaving the Pier 25 minigolf course, Ronan took me to a nearby restaurant, City Vineyard, where we enjoyed a leisurely meal of delicious wine and fresh seafood. Between the restaurant's rustic yet elegant wine-country décor and its spectacular views of the setting sun, which painted the waters of the Hudson River and the skyscrapers of Manhattan with a golden warmth, the setting could hardly have been more romantic.

The care he had taken in planning our outing moved me and heightened my awareness that with each passing day, I was falling deeper in love with him, a knowledge that periodically slammed into my gut and terrified me. If letting Ronan into my heart was a mistake, then it was one I couldn't take back, because when it came to my feelings for him, I'd passed the point of no return.

But right now, basking in the afterglow of what felt like our first true date, it seemed certain that Ronan was falling for me, too. Why else would he go to the trouble of planning an afternoon and evening so clearly intended for my pleasure?

Which was why, when we returned home, stepped into the privacy of our apartment, and Ronan closed the door behind us, I cupped his face in my hands and drew him into a tender kiss.

"Thank you for today," I said, tracing my fingers over his stubbled jawline. "You completely surprised me—and everything was beyond perfect."

His answering smile only reinforced my conviction that he returned my feelings.

"I'm glad you enjoyed our outing," he said. "After the wedding mania of the past few weeks, you deserve a break."

"So do you," I said, kissing him again, before taking his hand and tugging him toward the master bedroom. "But first, you need to lose your clothes."

He swept me off my feet and into his arms. "And let you tie me to the bed?"

I smiled at him. "We made a bet—and I won."

"You did," he said as he carried me toward the bedroom. "And I'm a man of my word. But before we do this, I need to tell you that letting you tie me up will be a new experience for me." He set me down on my feet in the middle of the bedroom. "I'm game to give it a shot—I just can't promise that I'll be into it."

Ronan's admission caught me by surprise, and I fixed him with a look. "You never expected me to win, did you? You expected to be the one tying me up—not the other way around."

"I did," he admitted. "And male anatomy being what it is, I'm concerned that I might not be able to…"

I finished his sentence. "Rise to the occasion?"

"Something like that."

When Ronan's confession sank into me, a sense of power tinged with mischief came over me. Tonight was my turn to take charge, and I knew exactly what I wanted to do to him.

I linked my hands behind his neck and looked him in the eye.

"Get naked," I said. "And trust me, by the time I'm done with you, you're definitely going to rise to *this* occasion."

# 31

## RONAN

Intrigued but nervous about what was to come, I began to remove my clothes, while Ava disappeared into her dressing room. When I was finished undressing, I lay down on the bed and waited for her to return.

When she did, she was as naked as I was, except for several flowing, colorful silk scarves draped around her neck. Despite my nervousness, my cock hardened at the sight of her.

She climbed onto the bed, straddled me, and we shared a heated, lingering kiss, before Ava tied one end of a translucent red scarf around my left wrist.

"That's not much of a restraint," I said, eying the delicate fabric. "I could easily rip it in half."

"Maybe you could," she said, her eyes sparkling with humor as she looped the other end of the scarf around the bedframe and knotted it firmly. "But then, you'd miss out on the meaning of doing this together."

"Which is?"

"Trust," she said, her expression turning serious. "And a kind of equality."

"What do you mean?"

"You're much physically stronger than I am," she said as she finished securing my other arm. "Because of your strength, when we make love, I trust you in ways that you don't have to trust me."

"I never thought of it that way," I said.

"Giving up control means trusting me with your pleasure," she said, moving down the bed to my feet. "It can be deeply erotic."

I gave her a skeptical look. "We'll see about that."

She tied a final knot and then climbed onto the bed and between my legs.

"Look at this," she said, eying my erection and shooting me a wicked look. "So much for performance anxiety."

She spoke the truth. My brain might not be fully on board, but the rest of me was ready to go, and when she dipped her head toward my crotch, I anticipated the velvety warmth of her mouth around my cock. Instead, she teased my balls with her lips and tongue in ways that made me crazy with lust, all the while lightly stroking my shaft with her hands.

As heat thrummed through my veins, I released a low groan and succumbed to the moment. When she ran her tongue up and down my cock and then sucked lightly on its base, my vision went black for a second. Forgetting my bonds, I reached for Ava, but the silk binding my wrists held my arms against the mattress.

"Ride me," I said. "Take me inside you."

"Soon," she said, her voice husky with desire. "But not yet."

She continued to tease me with her lips and tongue, pushing me to the brink of orgasm, driving me to heights of arousal I couldn't remember experiencing before.

Then, she straddled me and brushed the tip of my cock against her entrance, before leaning forward and running her fingertips through my hair, down the sides of my neck, and over my chest, exploring the muscles of my torso. Her light touch electrified my skin, and her breasts, tipped with the pert, rosy nipples I loved to play with, swung tantalizingly close to my face. I strained against my bonds, raising my head and shoulders as much as I could, trying to catch a nipple between my lips.

With both hands, Ava gently pushed my shoulders down against the pillows. "Relax," she said softly, her eyes dark and intense. "Trust me. Let me enjoy your body the way I let you enjoy mine."

"You're the boss," I said. "As long as I get my turn to tie you up later."

Her lips curved into a smile. "Do you ever stop negotiating?"

"No. It's part of my charm."

She layered kisses down my neck, before delivering a bite to my right nipple that sent a jolt of sensation straight to my cock. "We'll see," she said between kisses. "But not until I finish having my way with you."

She continued to tease me with kisses, nibbles, and caresses that kept me rock hard and craving more. Although part of me wanted to tear myself free from my bonds, seize Ava, and bury myself inside her, being her sex toy was fucking hot.

Her hands and mouth roamed my body, touching and tasting every part of me, while she used her own body to tease me, one moment exchanging a heated kiss, the next offering me a brush of her hardened nipples against my lips, or a taste of her slick folds.

When she finally positioned herself above me and guided my cock inside her, I groaned in ecstasy as, with deliberate slowness, she took me into herself, controlling the moment and prolonging it.

As my cock slid into her hot, wet perfection, a millimeter at a time, I gasped, overcome by the sensations that shot through my entire body.

Had anything in my life felt this amazing?

It hadn't.

And then she began to move. The sight of her riding me, with her dark hair flowing around her breasts, would have undone any man, and I was no exception. For an instant, she literally took my breath away, as her beauty and the intensity of the moment sucked the oxygen from the room.

When she sped up the pace, I arched against the mattress, straining against my bonds as my arousal heightened and my pulse went into overdrive.

"God, Ava," I groaned. "I'm going to come."

She shot me a meaningful look—and rode me harder.

Sensation arced through me, and a rushing sound filled my ears. Ava cried out, calling my name, just before my world exploded, shattered by the orgasm of a lifetime. Fireworks filled my vision, and when the room stopped turning around me, my body buzzed with the aftershocks of release. My heart still hammering against my chest, I drew in deep gulps of air as Ava freed my hands and feet, before stretching out on the bed beside me.

"Wow," I said, too stunned to formulate anything articulate. "Wow."

Ava gave me a satisfied look. "Despite your skepticism, it seems you enjoy light bondage."

I pulled her into my arms. "What I enjoy is having my cock inside you. Being tied up had nothing to do with it."

She pressed a kiss against the tip of my nose. "Are you sure about that?"

"Of course I'm sure...well, mostly sure. In any case, you deserve all the credit."

She ran her palm down my abs and then over my cock, before smiling at me. "Let's just say you inspire me."

As I gazed into her eyes, something twinged inside me. Ava was an amazing woman, a loyal friend, and an incredible lover. For a brief moment, I wished I were a better man. The kind of man who deserved a woman like her by my side, the kind of man who could trust himself to treat her like the treasure she was.

But then I pushed that thought aside. I was who I was, and right now, it was good to be me. I was exactly where I wanted to be.

I cupped Ava's breasts and teased her nipples. "Time for

payback," I said, giving her a suggestive look. "Now it's my turn to tie you to the bed."

She laughed and held out her slender wrists to me. "Go ahead," she said. "I'm all yours."

"That's right," I said as I reached for one of the silk scarves that were strewn across the foot of the bed. "Tonight, you're all mine."

## 32

### AVA

"The wedding's only eight days away," Mimi said. She sipped her coffee, eyeing me over the cup. "How are you holding up—and how's your new arrangement with Ronan working out?"

"Everything's fine, I guess. It's just all more than a little confusing."

It was Friday morning, and we were sitting in Mimi's jewelry studio, drinking coffee at the battered workbench where she brought her creations to life. With the wedding arrangements completed, I was finally able to catch my breath—but having time to think was also forcing me to acknowledge my deepening feelings for Ronan.

"What do you mean?" Mimi asked. "Confusing in what way?"

"Ronan's giving me mixed signals. His words tell me that he thinks of us as friends with benefits—but his actions send a different message."

"Give me some examples," Mimi said.

"When we worked out our new arrangement, we agreed to maintain separate bedrooms."

"I remember," Mimi said. "Sleeping separately from him was one of the ways you hoped to keep some emotional distance."

"It was—and initially, Ronan went along with it. He didn't seem to care. But now, after we make love in his bed, if I try to return to my room, he finds a way to get me to stay. And when I wake up in the morning, he's wrapped around me."

"So it's not just about sex anymore."

"It certainly doesn't feel that way. I haven't forgotten about his history of dating half of Manhattan, but what we have together feels real."

"People can change," Mimi said. "Even playboys like Ronan Kingsley."

"Last Saturday, he surprised me by taking me out on a date, followed up by a night of incredible sex."

Her face brightened, and she reached for the vintage tin where she kept her weed supply and rolling papers. "You have to tell me everything—but before you start, I'm going to roll myself one mother of a joint, which will only enhance my vicarious pleasure."

"How the hell do you do it?" I said as she dipped her fingers into the tin and then crumbled a thick line of green leaves onto the rolling paper. "How do you smoke the way you do without ever seeming to get high? It's a mystery to me."

She winked at me. "Thirty years of practice. I'm a well-adjusted hippie girl."

Her nimble fingers made quick work of rolling the joint, which she stuck between her lips, before using a hot-pink lighter to ignite its tip. She inhaled deeply before blowing smoke toward the ceiling and fixing her gaze on me. "Now, tell me everything. And don't you dare leave out the sexy bits."

I told her, and when I explained the bet that had resulted in Ronan letting me tie him up, she laughed out loud.

"Ronan's a good sport," she said, taking a drag on her joint. "I like that in a man. And actions speak louder than words. Do you think he's falling in love with you?"

"Maybe I'm reading too much into it, but our relationship doesn't feel like friends with benefits. It feels like more."

"Do you want it to be more?" she asked.

After a long moment, I met her gaze and admitted the truth. "I do. I've tried to keep my emotional distance, but my feelings just keep getting stronger, and I need to know if he feels the same way. Based on his behavior, I believe he does—but if he doesn't, I need to take a huge step back."

"From the sex?"

"And everything that goes with it—the intimate conversations, the constant touching, and all the other gestures that make me feel like he's falling in love with me, just as I am with him."

"Have you talked with him about this?"

"Not yet," I said. "But I intend to."

"When?"

"Soon. Either this week, before the wedding, or the week afterward, when Ronan gains access to his trust and things settle down."

"What does Cara think of all this?" Mimi asked.

"Cara's sure that Ronan's in love with me—and she couldn't be more thrilled. She has visions of our fake marriage becoming real. But she also said that he needs time to acknowledge his feelings and advised me not to rush things between us, which is why I'm considering waiting to talk to him until after the wedding, when we're both under less stress."

"I disagree," Mimi said. "You and Ronan need to come clean with each other before your wedding day. When the two of you speak your vows, you both deserve to know what the words coming out of your mouths mean—or don't mean."

"I hadn't thought of it that way," I said. "But you're right."

"You can't put this off," she said. "When the two of you go into this wedding, you both need to be clear on exactly what you're doing and why."

"I won't put it off," I reassured her. "Sometime in the next few days, I'll find the right moment."

Mimi leveled me with a look. "There is no perfect moment, Ava. Don't overthink this."

I rolled my eyes. "You know me. I overthink everything—I can't help myself."

"Just keep one thing in mind," she said.

"What's that?"

"Ronan could be in the same position as you. What if his feelings for you have deepened, but he's unsure of how you feel about him?"

"I suppose that's possible."

She smiled at me. "It's never easy to make the first move. But someone has to."

## 33

### AVA

Later that afternoon, I was sitting at my desk at Oasis, putting the finishing touches on my presentation for a potential client that Ronan had sent my way. He'd kept his word about helping me with my business, another way in which we'd become a team.

An amazing team.

I smiled to myself, recalling our rough beginning, when it had seemed like we argued about every other thing. Due to our strong personalities, we still clashed occasionally, but when it came to the important stuff, we were usually in agreement.

Ronan was a linear thinker, and while it sometimes felt like he oversimplified everything, he was fabulous at cutting through the noise to reach the heart of a matter. And once he'd grasped that my world view wasn't totally alien to his own—it just had far more shades of gray—we'd been able to talk easily about everything under the sun.

Well, almost everything. We hadn't yet talked about our feelings for each other—but I was gearing up for that conversation. Sometime within the next day or two, I'd find the right moment to tell Ronan how deeply I'd come to care for him.

Just then, the door opened, and I was stunned to see Veronica Kingsley enter the room. Her heels clicked against the hardwood floor as she strode briskly toward my desk. Dressed in a flowing navy silk pantsuit accessorized with pearls, she appeared more polished than ever against the battered walls and used furnishings of my rented workspace.

"Hello, Ava," she said. "We need to talk."

Why was she here? Was she about to drop some new, wedding-related bombshell—and if so, why had she bothered coming to my workplace, instead of calling or dropping by the apartment?

I rose to greet her. "Good afternoon, Veronica. Can I get you a cup of coffee, or tea?"

"That won't be necessary," she said. "What I have to say won't take long."

With an expression of distaste, she perched on the battered red bucket chair that I thought of as Mimi's and positioned her purse on her knees.

I sat back down at my desk, shut my laptop, and gave her my full attention.

"What do we need to discuss?" I asked.

"Your upcoming marriage to my stepson," she said. "It's a fake, a ruse to gain access to his trust money—and we both know it."

For a moment, I just stared at her as my mind raced. Could she possibly know the truth about my arrangement with Ronan? It didn't seem possible. Aside from Ronan and me, only Cara, Mimi, and Jack knew the truth, and none of them would sell us out.

Which meant that Veronica had to be bluffing. No other explanation made sense.

"Where is this coming from?" I said. "Ronan and I love each other."

She raised an eyebrow at me. "Cut the little-miss-perfect act. It doesn't fool me for a minute. Your sudden engagement was suspicious from day one, and now, thanks to Aiden, I know all about Ronan's financial problems."

"Whatever you've heard is malicious gossip," I said. "Ronan's business is thriving."

She rolled her eyes. "Spare me the lies."

I didn't know what else to do, so I threw everything I had at her. "Believe what you want, Veronica. I don't need to convince you of anything. Ronan and I love each other, and one week from tomorrow, we'll be married. Nothing you say or do can stop us."

She eyed me with grudging respect. "So that's how you want to play it?" She reached into her purse. "How much do you want?"

I stared at her. "What?"

She pulled out a checkbook and waved it at me. "Money. How much is Ronan paying you? A million—or two? Whatever the amount, I'm prepared to outbid him."

A cold fury rushed through me. Who did she think she was? How could she whip out her checkbook and play God with Ronan's life?

When I regained control of myself, I stared the bitch down and asked the question that had plagued me from the day I'd first met her.

"Why do you hate Ronan so much?"

"What does that have to do with anything?"

"So there it is—you do hate him. You just admitted it."

"I admitted nothing. You heard what you wanted to hear."

"I heard the truth from your own lips—and I expect an explanation."

"Very well," Veronica said. "I don't particularly like either of my stepchildren, but I don't hate them, either. I'm only doing what's necessary to ensure that Aiden receives the inheritance he deserves."

Her statement was in line with Cara's belief that Veronica's aim was to make sure that Aiden received the bulk of Carter Kingsley's fortune, at Ronan and Cara's expense.

"Carter's a billionaire," I said. "He has a wife and three children. Isn't a quarter of his fortune enough for each of you? Why are you so determined to get Ronan disinherited?"

"It's not that simple," she said. "Carter won't divide the firm. He'll leave Kingsley Capital to one of his two sons, just as his father left it to him."

"And you want Aiden to inherit Kingsley Capital."

"Of course I do," Veronica said. "The firm is worth more than the total of Carter's other assets, and right now, Carter intends that it go to Ronan—his eldest son. Compared to what Ronan will inherit, my son gets a pittance."

"A quarter of Carter's other assets is no pittance—and Carter's old-fashioned attitude in favoring his eldest son isn't fair to Cara, either."

"Cara doesn't count. Carter would never leave his business to a woman."

"That's outrageous."

She shrugged. "I don't disagree, but that's the way it is. One of Carter's two sons will get Kingsley Capital, and I intend to make sure that son is Aiden. If Ronan's business fails, Carter will be embarrassed by that failure, and I'll be able to convince him to alter his will in Aiden's favor. Carter won't risk leaving Kingsley Capital to a son with poor business judgment—a son who might destroy his legacy."

For the first time, I fully grasped not only Veronica's aim but also her thinking. In a twisted way, she no doubt saw herself as a mother fighting for her child. But in her vicious quest to seize money and power for her son, greed had led her to pit brother against brother, and to tear the Kingsley family apart in the process.

"This has been your plan all along, hasn't it?" I said. "This is why you put Ronan down at every turn, always trying to make him look bad to Carter."

"What if I have?" she said. "When Aiden inherits the Kingsley fortune and the place in society that goes with it, his success will be worth everything I've done to assure it."

Her words sickened me. After growing up surrounded by Carter's prejudice and Veronica's machinations, it was a miracle that Ronan and Cara had turned out to be the kind, decent people who they were.

"Put your checkbook away," I said. "I understand that you love Aiden and want the best for him—but I love Ronan and would never do anything to hurt him. Carter's will may not be fair, but ultimately, it's his right to leave Kingsley Capital to whoever he chooses—and regardless of who he chooses, each of his children will still inherit a fortune."

Veronica leaned forward in her chair. "You're making a mistake, Ava. I'm prepared to offer you two million dollars to call off this farce of a wedding." She gestured at my less-than-impressive office space. "With that kind of money, you could rent a space in Manhattan and set up a real business for yourself."

My blood simmered. "My business may not be worth millions, but there are some things money can't buy, and one of them is my heart. I would never betray the man I love."

Her eyes narrowed. "Three million, then, you gold-digging upstart."

Fighting to contain my rising anger, I leveled her with a look. "Why is it so difficult for you to accept the truth? Ronan and I are getting married because we're in love, and no amount of money will change that reality."

She scrutinized me for several seconds before emitting a brittle laugh. "Silly girl. You've fallen for him, haven't you?"

"Veronica, we're in love. It's high time you faced that fact."

"If you think Ronan loves you, you're a fool. He's just like his father."

I glared at her, resisting the urge to reach across the desk and slap her perfectly made-up face. "Ronan's nothing like his father."

She regarded me with contempt. "Don't be stupid. Ronan's a skirt-chaser, just like Carter. Neither of them love anyone or anything beyond their own pleasure."

At that, something snapped inside me, and I stood up from my chair. "You need to leave, and leave now. You've made your disgusting offer, and you've heard my response. There's nothing more for us to say to each other."

Veronica got to her feet, slung her purse over her shoulder, and stalked toward the door. But when she reached it, she paused and turned back to me.

"Call me if you change your mind," she said evenly. "My offer's good until the day before the wedding."

"Whatever. I won't be calling."

"You'll live to regret this."

"I'll never regret turning down your filthy bribe."

It was then that Veronica delivered her most spiteful shot.

"One day you will," she said. "And it won't be your only regret, because you're betting your future on the wrong man. Ronan doesn't love you—and he never will."

## 34

### RONAN

When I returned home from work and entered my apartment, I couldn't have been in better spirits. With the wedding eight days away and the preparations for it completed, I was looking forward to a relaxed weekend with Ava. Tonight, I intended to suggest ordering takeout and then watching a movie together, an activity that inevitably led to making out on the couch, a perfect prelude to taking Ava to my bed and having my way with her.

"Hi, princess," I called jokingly as I closed the door behind me. "I'm home."

"In the kitchen," Ava called back.

As I left the foyer, crossed the living room, and entered the kitchen, the scent of cinnamon reached my nostrils. A sheet of what looked like molasses cookies rested on the stovetop, and Ava was removing a second sheet from the oven.

After she closed and turned off the oven, she faced me.

"You're not going to believe what happened today," she said. "I'm still stunned by it myself."

"Tell me," I said as I reached for a cookie.

"Veronica stopped by my office."

My stepmother was nothing if not relentlessly interfering, so while the news that she had interrupted Ava's work was unwelcome, it wasn't exactly surprising. But with the wedding invitations sent, and contracts signed with the caterers and florists, it wasn't like Veronica could change anything major—although she'd no doubt been her usual bitchy self.

"Sorry your day got interrupted," I said, biting into my cookie, which was delicious. "I hope her visit wasn't too awful."

"She offered me three million bucks to break up with you."

I nearly choked and swallowed hard to recover. "What the hell?"

"I turned her down, of course," Ava said.

As my pulse—which had shot through the roof—settled down, Ava's matter-of-fact rejection of Veronica's offer sank into me.

"There's no 'of course' about turning down that kind of money," I said.

She furrowed her brow. "There is for me. I would never betray you."

Maybe she took that kind of loyalty for granted—but I didn't. Not after growing up with my father's detachment and my stepmother's deceit.

I pulled her into my arms. "From day one, you've always had my back, which means more than you know. But since Veronica can't stop our marriage, there's no need to worry."

She wrapped her arms around my waist and rested her head against my chest. "How can you be so calm about your stepmother trying to ruin you?"

"Practice," I said, dropping a kiss on the top of her head. "She's been trying to ruin me for years."

Ava leaned back and tilted her face toward mine, her gaze intense with concern. "Then you know it's just a matter of time before she tries again. She's hell-bent on Aiden getting Kingsley Capital and the bulk of your father's fortune."

I released her. "Veronica's ambitions for Aiden are nothing new, and I for one don't care if she achieves them, as long as it doesn't interfere with the success of my own business."

Ava looked surprised. "You don't care if you inherit your father's firm?"

"I don't. Why do you think I started Kingsley Tech instead of going to work for my father?"

"The same reasons I started Oasis," she said. "Independence, and doing what you love."

"Those factors played a role, but here's the primary reason. Years ago, I made the decision not to base my life on speculating about the future of my father's money. Whatever he leaves me—or doesn't leave me—is his decision, and there's no point in thinking about it, let alone worrying about it. It's beyond my control."

"Most people expect to inherit whatever they consider to be their fair share of their parents' money, even when there's not much to spread around."

I shrugged and reached for a second cookie. "I'm not most people, and obsessing about my father's intentions is a waste of energy. I'd rather focus on doing my own thing—which, right now, means ordering takeout, instead of eating an entire sheet of these cookies, which are delicious."

"My grandmother's recipe never fails," Ava said with a smile. "What do you feel like eating tonight?"

"How about Saigon Shack? I could go for some beef pho."

"Sold," she said. "I love their spring rolls."

"And since I picked the food—"

"I pick the movie. While you call in our order, I'll look for something good on Netflix."

I leaned forward and kissed her on the lips. "Let's forget about my stepmother, OK? Fuck letting her invade our movie night."

She kissed me back. "Agreed. Movie nights are sacred."

After dinner, we settled down on the couch to watch the movie Ava had chosen, *Bringing Up Baby*.

"This seems vaguely familiar," I said when Cary Grant appeared on the television screen. "Cary looks even more wussy than usual in those dumb-looking glasses."

"Even old-fashioned glasses can't touch Cary's studliness," Ava said. "Besides, he's supposed to be a stuffy paleontologist."

"I suppose that explains the glasses."

"And Katherine Hepburn's a flighty socialite with a pet leopard. If you've seen the movie before, we can watch something else."

I cocked my head at her. "Since your description doesn't ring a bell, my sense of familiarity must be due to Cary's frequent appearances on my TV screen."

Ava rolled her eyes. "Since when have I denied my Cary obsession? Get ready to laugh your ass off. *Bringing Up Baby* is the best screwball comedy ever."

With Ava curled against me and a glass of Scotch in my hand, a sense of contentment crept over me as together, we spent the next hour and a half watching and laughing at what had to be one of the most ridiculous romantic comedies ever made. When the screen faded to black from Grant and Hepburn's final embrace, Ava turned to me, her face glowing with happiness.

"Thank you for indulging me," she said. "After my run-in with she-who-shall-not-be-named, I needed this."

I drained the remainder of my Scotch and set the glass on the coffee table, anticipating the next stage of the evening. We'd talk, relax, and make out on the couch a bit, before heading for the comfort of my bed to have our way with each other.

"My pleasure," I said. "Once the wedding's behind us, hopefully we'll be able to enjoy evenings like this more often."

"I'd like that," she said. "Speaking of our wedding, there's something I wanted to talk to you about."

"What's on your mind?"

"Us," she said. "How do you think we're doing?"

After her encounter with Veronica, Ava no doubt needed a little reassurance, and after turning down three million bucks for me, she deserved all the support I could give her.

"As far as I'm concerned, things couldn't be better. When we signed our marriage agreement, I was skeptical about whether it could really work out, but at this point, I feel incredibly lucky."

"What were you skeptical about, early on?"

"Sharing an apartment, and giving up sex." I gave her a suggestive look. "Although as it turned out, it didn't take you long to put the moves on me."

She laughed. "According to my recollection, you seduced me."

"Not my fault." I reached for her hand, lifted it to my lips, and kissed it. "You're irresistible."

As she met my gaze, the laughter faded from her face, and her expression turned serious. Somber, even. Had I said something wrong? Or had Veronica's attempted bribery shaken her more than I'd realized?

"I feel the same way about you," she said. "Which is why we need to talk. When we agreed to our marriage arrangement, it was all about saving our respective businesses. We barely knew each other, and we couldn't even be sure if we would get along as roommates."

"I remember wondering about that, too," I said, unsure where she was going. "But those days are far behind us."

"First, we became friends," she said. "Then, the night of our engagement party, we became lovers."

I squeezed her hand. "Best decision we ever made."

"I hope so," she said. "Because making love with you, getting closer to you—it's shown me who you really are and what our life together could be. I know you feel something for me—the way you respond to me tells me that much—but before we go through with this wedding, I need to tell you that I'm in love with you. With each taste of you, I want more, and with each passing day, my feelings for you deepen."

As the significance of Ava's words sank into me, my brain froze.

She couldn't really be in love with me—could she? The last thing I wanted was to hurt her, but telling her what she wanted to hear wasn't an option. Because while I liked Ava tremendously and lusted after her constantly, I wasn't in love with her.

And I couldn't lie to her either.

"I care about you, Ava. You know I do. There's nothing fake about our friendship or about how much I enjoy being with you."

Her hand trembled in mine, before she quickly withdrew it and stood to her feet. When she spoke, her voice was flat. "There's no need to go on. I get the message."

"This has nothing to do with you," I said. "You're an amazing person. But I've never been in love with anyone, and I don't expect I ever will be. I'm just not wired that way."

Her lips tightened, and I sensed that she was battling back tears. "Don't bother trying to let me down easy, Ronan. My feelings are what they are. So are yours."

"I never meant to hurt you, and I'm sorry that I have." Unable to bear the pain written on her face, I got to my feet, walked to the living-room window, and stared out at the night sky. "This is my fault—and I don't even begin to know how to fix it."

"Not everything can be fixed," Ava said quietly. "And it's more my fault than yours. But calling off the wedding would only make things worse for both of us, so if you're worried that I'm about to go there, don't be. I'm disappointed and sad, not stupid."

Relief and guilt warred inside me. Relief that she was still willing to go through with the wedding, and guilt that despite her turning down Veronica's money, which would have been three times more than I was paying her, I couldn't be the man she wanted me to be.

"Thank you for standing by me," I said. "Although right now, I don't feel like I deserve that kind of loyalty."

"You deserve to keep the business you've worked hard to build. But let's be clear. Our physical intimacy is over. We need to return to our original arrangement."

I'd seen that one coming, but it still cut deep. "Understood. Although I hope we can still be friends."

"Maybe someday. Right now, I need time to clear my head. I'll do my best to get there, but you'll probably have to wait."

I turned back to face her. "Deep down, you know I'm not right for you. Someday, after our fake marriage is over, you'll find a man who'll love you the way you deserve to be loved, and when you find him, no one will be happier for you than me. But the next two years will be easier on both of us if we find a way to get along."

"You've made your point about trying to remain friends, and I agree with you. But that doesn't change the fact that right now, I want a lot more than friendship from you. And as much as I wish I could, I can't just switch those feelings off."

"Is there anything I can do?"

"Yes, Ronan. Between now and the wedding, give me my space and leave me alone."

And with that, she turned away, walked into her bedroom, and shut the door firmly behind her.

# 35

## AVA

After I closed the door of my bedroom, I leaned against it, trembling from the effort of containing the storm of emotions raging through me.

How could I have been so stupid? Why was I such a goddamned fool?

I'd read Ronan all wrong. Sure, he liked me well enough—especially in bed—but Veronica's cruel words had turned out to be true. He didn't love me, and he never would.

As I stepped to the daybed and slumped onto it, hot tears slid from my eyes and streaked down my cheeks. A lump formed in my throat, and as the ache in my chest burned and expanded, I grabbed a large throw pillow and smashed my face into it, muffling my ragged gasps and the raw, torn sobs that escaped my lips. Maybe I couldn't help crying over the loss of my misguided, hopeless dream of building a life with Ronan, but I hadn't broken down in front of him, and the last thing I wanted was for him to hear me wailing in misery.

I still had my pride.

It was all I had left—so I clung to it like the life preserver that it was and rode out the storm.

When it finally passed, I remained on the daybed, my face still buried in the pillow. But after a few minutes, I sat up, wiped my eyes, and came to a decision. Before trying to sleep, I would take a shower.

I couldn't wash Ronan out of my heart, but I could wash his touch from my skin.

I got to my feet and slowly undressed myself, before going into the bathroom and turning the hot water to a near-scalding temperature. After I stepped into the shower, I washed and rinsed my hair, before scrubbing every inch of my body. As I washed myself, my tears blended with the shower's hot spray, and my heart throbbed with grief.

But by the time I toweled myself dry, found an oversized T-shirt to sleep in, and made up the daybed with sheets and a duvet, my emotions shifted from agony into disbelief.

How could I have misread Ronan so completely?

Had I focused too much on the powerful chemistry that pulled us together and not enough on who he really was? Or had I deluded myself and seen only what I wanted to see in him, the same mistake I'd made with my ex-fiancé?

In any case, if I was honest with myself, this disaster was my fault. I couldn't blame Ronan, and he didn't deserve to pay the price for my stupidity. By telling him to leave me alone, I'd ended tonight's conversation on a harsher note than I'd meant to—but maybe it was for the best. With the wedding a week away, I desperately needed time and space to adjust to my new reality.

How had I ended up here? Where had I gone wrong?

I'd agreed to marry Ronan to save my business, but at this point, it wasn't about Oasis anymore. No amount of money could possibly be worth spending the next two years of my life in this kind of pain. But if there was any escape from marrying Ronan and living with him for the next two years, I couldn't see it, because even if I was ready to sacrifice my own business, without our marriage, he would lose his business too.

And I couldn't do that to him. I had to keep my commitment, which meant that somehow I needed to give up my foolish dreams of building a life with Ronan, pick up the pieces of my shattered heart, and move on.

But how was I supposed to move on when I had to live with him for the next two fucking years?

I slipped between the sheets, switched off the light, and pulled the blanket up to my ears. Darkness and silence surrounded me, and as I rested my now-aching head against the pillow, my limited options pressed in on me like a vise.

All I could do was keep as much distance from Ronan as possible and do my best to get through one day at a time.

Which brought me back to the most immediate question.

How the hell was I going to survive the wedding?

# 36

## RONAN

Over the next few days, Ava spent most of the time closeted in her room. Whenever she emerged, I did my best to act normal, and she responded politely to whatever I said, but it was as if a glass wall had descended between us.

After several days of near-silence, one morning when she was making a pot of coffee, I joined her in the kitchen and made an attempt to reach out to her.

"That coffee smells good," I said.

She reached into a cupboard, took down a mug, filled it, and placed it on the counter beside me. "Here you go."

"Thank you."

"You're welcome." She filled a second cup for herself and headed toward her room.

"Can we talk for a minute?" I said.

She turned back to me. "Of course. What do you want to talk about?"

"You. Me. This…situation we're in. Before, it felt like we were in it together—and now, it feels like we're each on our own. I miss our friendship."

A shadow of pain crossed her face. "I'm sorry," she said quietly. "But you'll have to talk to someone else about that. I know I'm not being a very good friend right now, but I'm doing the best I can."

"We can't go on like this," I said. "Living in the same apartment and barely speaking."

"Things between us have changed."

"I'm not pretending they haven't. But we can't go on being this uncomfortable around each other."

She regarded me thoughtfully. "You have a point. I don't feel like talking, but how about watching the morning news together?"

"Let's do it."

She walked into the living room, stepped to the coffee table, picked up the remote, and switched on CNN. After I sat down in my favorite armchair, she seated herself on the end of the couch furthest from me and fixed her attention on the television screen.

As Wolf Blitzer droned on about North Korea, I watched Ava out of the corner of my vision, wishing that I could join her on the couch like I used to. Sure, I wanted to fuck her—my desire for her was stronger than ever—but right now, I would have happily settled for holding her hand or feeling her head rest against my shoulder.

But by being honest about who I was, I'd stepped up and taken the consequences like a man. Before, when I'd convinced Ava to sleep with me, the thought that she might develop feelings for me hadn't crossed my mind. I'd always attracted debutantes and party girls like flies, but never a woman like Ava, who deserved a better man than I'd ever be.

My recklessness had damaged our friendship, but I wouldn't let that happen again. In time, she'd understand that I'd done the right thing for both of us and thank me for it.

But in the meantime, watching the news together was progress.

And right now, I'd take whatever I could get.

# 37

## AVA

By the morning of the day of the wedding, I had reached a numbed acceptance of what I needed to do.

I'd put on the wedding dress that I'd selected with so much hope and wore it with a smile on my face, even though Ronan's rejection had burned my heart to ash. I'd stand before the Southampton elite and speak fake vows, even though I still wanted to believe in the words that would emerge from my lips. And I'd smile my way through an elaborate reception and dinner, even though I craved to be alone.

Over the past week, I'd done my best to avoid Ronan, crawl under the emotional equivalent of a rock, and lick my wounds, but nothing could ease the pain in my heart, a pain that was only worsened by Ronan's well-meaning efforts to make it up to me.

Which, at the moment, included borrowing his father's helicopter and pilot to fly us from the downtown Manhattan heliport to

Southampton, a gesture that would have thrilled me just a week ago—but now only made me ache for what might have been.

Why couldn't he go back to being the arrogant dickhead with whom I'd contracted this crazy fake-marriage agreement? Couldn't he see that each act of thoughtfulness just drove another knife into my heart?

As Ronan helped me into the helicopter, before handing me the boxes containing our wedding clothes, I checked my wave of self-pity.

I'd gotten myself into this mess. I'd gone into it with my eyes open. Agreeing to a fake marriage had been a gamble, and giving in to my desire for Ronan had been another.

I'd gambled knowingly—and I'd lost.

Now, I had to pay the price for that loss, and through the seven circles of hell that stretched before me, I needed to maintain as much dignity as I could muster. Which, today, meant plastering a big fake smile on my face and doing my best to look and act like the happiest woman on earth.

As I settled into one of the helicopter's luxurious leather-upholstered bucket seats, Ronan handed me a headset with large ear cushions and an attached mic. When he did, our fingers touched for the briefest of instants, and the spark that shot through me told me—as if I needed any reminding—just how much I still craved his every look and touch.

*Fuck my life.*

Forcing my face into a neutral expression, I slipped the headset over my ears, anticipating the respite that the forty-minute flight to Southampton seemed likely to provide. While our headsets would cancel much of the engine noise, being on the same communication channel as the pilot limited our ability to speak freely—a limitation for which I was grateful. If I was going to get through today, I needed to seize every second of quiet that I could.

The pilot started up the engines, which whined, hummed, and screeched as the rotors began to spin. As their spinning sped up, the whup-whup sound I associated with helicopters emerged from the noise.

The pilot's voice came over my headphones. "Prepare for takeoff."

Seconds later, the helicopter lifted from the ground and banked toward the ocean. As we picked up speed, the city's looming skyscrapers shrank away beyond my window.

As Manhattan receded into the distance, I chanced a sidelong glance at Ronan, who sat across from me, looking out the opposite window. Dressed for the flight in jeans, a leather bomber jacket, and aviator sunglasses, he was impossibly handsome, and I couldn't help wishing that things could have turned out differently between us.

Pushing away the grief that threatened to overwhelm me, I turned back to the window, fixed my gaze on the horizon, and forced myself to take a deep breath. I couldn't afford to give way to my feelings, and dwelling on what could have been wouldn't help me get through the day I faced.

Just then, the helicopter emitted a coughing sound and lurched to the left, throwing me against the right arm of my seat. For an instant, terror arced through my veins, before the engine sound shifted back to normal, and the aircraft righted itself.

"Sorry," the pilot said. "One of the engines cut out for a second—but it's fine now. Anyway, this bird's a twin-engine, so there's nothing to fear."

Ronan leaned forward in his seat and spoke into the mic on his headset. "Ava—are you all right?"

"I'm fine," I said as I readjusted my own headset, which had slipped off one ear.

"There's nothing to worry about," he said. "Even if we lost one of the two engines—which we haven't—this copter flies perfectly well on one."

"Thanks," I said, meaning it. "That makes me feel safer."

"You and me both," he said with a reassuring smile. "Although for a few seconds there, I was wishing I'd asked for Dad's limo instead."

Relieved that the helicopter was fine, I smiled back. "You and me both—but if you had, we'd still be sitting in traffic, instead of halfway to Southampton."

"True," he said. "Now that spring has arrived, I'm sure traffic's bumper-to-bumper much of the way."

Throughout the rest of the flight, which passed without incident, Ronan and I sat in companionable silence, and when we approached Southampton, I felt more confident about my ability to handle the day to come.

I wasn't fully myself, and I couldn't expect to be flying high anytime soon. But like an aircraft chugging along on one engine instead of two, I was getting by. I was doing what I'd committed to do and what needed to be done to save Ronan's business.

And one step at a time, I would survive this wedding.

## 38

### RONAN

When the helicopter landed at the Southampton estate, Veronica rushed Ava and me to the third-floor bedrooms, where we would change and prepare for the wedding. Since Ava and I had opted for an afternoon wedding, I'd chosen to wear a charcoal-gray morning suit and a white shirt, together with a pale silver vest and tie.

I had nearly finished dressing and was fiddling with my cufflinks when someone knocked on the door.

"Come in," I called, expecting Jack, who was to be my best man.

But when the door opened, my brother, Aiden, entered, wearing a fitted dark suit and an awkward expression.

"Do you have a few minutes?" he said. "We need to talk."

"A few," I said, working my second cufflink into place. "But you'll need to make it quick, because Veronica's expecting me downstairs in half an hour, and you know how she is."

Aiden closed the door behind him before turning toward me. "I used to think I understood my mother better than anyone. Now, I'm not so sure."

I finished securing the cufflink and began to put on my tie. "What do you mean?"

"I overheard her talking to her friend Marianne about her plans to break up you and Ava—and later, I questioned her about what I'd heard."

I stopped what I was doing and looked my brother in the eye. "Then you know that Veronica offered Ava three million bucks to break up with me."

Aiden's face flushed. "I do—and I want you to know that I had nothing to do with it. You and I might not get along, but I would never fuck with your personal life."

He seemed sincere, and my gut said that he was being honest with me.

"Don't worry about it," I said. "The wedding's still on, and in any case, you're not responsible for your mother's actions."

Aiden looked relieved. "Thank you for saying that."

"It's a simple fact," I said mildly. "As is the reality that your mother desperately wants you to inherit Kingsley Capital."

Aiden's gaze darkened. "I don't need anyone's help to succeed, and I've told my mother to stop interfering with my plans."

My expression must have revealed my surprise, because Aiden released a dry chuckle. "Looks like I've shocked you."

"Frankly, you have. Are you considering leaving the firm?"

"Not at the moment—but in another year or so. Dad's approach is more conservative than mine, and once I get a bit more experience under my belt, I plan on starting my own business, just like you did. By the time I'm Dad's age, I intend to run one of the most successful investment firms on Wall Street, and when I get there, no one's going to be able to say that I did it by stealing my brother's legacy."

I looked at my brother with new respect. His statement brought back memories of my own youthful rebelliousness and ambition, as did the fire with which he'd spoken. Was Aiden finally growing up and becoming his own person instead of his mother's pawn?

"Dad's a piece of work," I said. "As far as I'm concerned, he can leave Kingsley Capital to whoever he wants. I've got my own business, and I refuse to participate in head games that pit family members against each other."

"I feel the same way," Aiden said. "Anyway, you won't have to worry about my mother's interference going forward. I've shut that problem down for good."

Was it possible that he had? Without questioning him, I couldn't begin to know—but in taking on Veronica, Aiden had stepped up for me, and I needed to treat him like the man he was trying to become.

Which meant not cross-examining him. Which meant showing him respect—and trust.

So I held out my hand to him. "Thank you for talking to Veronica."

Aiden shook my hand with a firm grip. "I just wish I'd found out what she was up to in time to stop her from dragging Ava into our fucked-up family drama." His lips quirked in a wry half smile. "But I suppose the silver lining is knowing what your future wife is made of."

"I'm a lucky man," I said, wishing for the first time that I didn't have to lie to my brother about my marriage, that I could reciprocate the honesty with which he'd just spoken to me. But I couldn't. At least not now and definitely not without talking it through with Ava.

"You're beyond lucky," Aiden said. "Shit, she turned down a three-million-dollar bribe for you." He shook his head. "She must really love you."

"She does," I said, being as truthful as I could. "And take it from me, it's a humbling experience."

My brother furrowed his brow at me. "What do you mean?"

"Being loved like that. I can't possibly deserve it."

"Maybe you don't deserve Ava, maybe you do," Aiden said. "I'm certainly in no position to judge or give advice, beyond what I've learned from growing up in our messed-up family."

When he hesitated, I met his gaze. "Go on."

"You can't change the past. But your future is up to you. If Ava deserves a better man, maybe you should just do your best to be that guy."

For a long moment, I just looked at Aiden's face, which radiated good intentions. In time, my younger brother would learn one of life's harshest lessons, which was that people didn't change. In small ways, sure—but not when it came to stuff that really mattered. At the end of the day, I'd always known I was a Kingsley and my father's son. Sure, I'd tried to be more honest about who I was. I'd tried to find a way to be myself without hurting anyone.

And what had my efforts accomplished? I'd hurt Ava, and I'd told a shit ton of lies to support the fake marriage that was about to take place. A better man would have found another way to save his business. A better way. One that didn't involve lying or hurting people.

But I wasn't that man, and I hadn't found a better way.

Which meant I had a wedding to get through. So, despising myself for doing it, I put a smile on my face and clapped my brother on the back, faking a lightheartedness I wished I could feel. "Thanks, Aiden—I'll keep that in mind. Now, I'd better get my ass downstairs."

"Before you're late for your own wedding?" he joked.

"You got it," I said, winking at him. "Keeping my beautiful bride waiting isn't an option."

# 39

## AVA

After Cara helped me into my wedding gown and zipped its back, I gazed into the mirrored vanity in the bedroom suite that had been set up as my dressing room, part of me still not fully believing the reflection that stared back at me. The Vera Wang dress we'd chosen for me was a lovely balance of modern and classic. Ivory and sleeveless, with a deep V neckline exposed just enough cleavage, its skirt fanned out gracefully from my waistline, and appliques of delicate, corded lace added a touch of shimmer to its classic silhouette. I'd styled my dark hair in a sleek updo, which complemented the clean lines of my dress, and diamond solitaire earrings sparkled from my ears, completing my look.

    Aside from a trace of shadows beneath my eyes, I looked every bit the perfect Hamptons bride, and aside from Cara and Mimi, who knew that I'd bared my heart to Ronan and been rejected, no one would see the truth behind the illusion, let alone what it was costing me to maintain it.

"We definitely picked the right dress," Cara said, stepping back to inspect me. "You're gorgeous, and you'll only be more stunning when I finish your makeup." She glanced around. "Damn it. I must have left my makeup bag in my room."

"Can't we use mine? Trust me, it's fully stocked with everything we could possibly need."

"My brushes are better than your brushes."

I rolled my eyes. "That's a matter of opinion."

"Back in two minutes," she said, heading for the door.

When it closed behind her, I nervously paced back and forth, as the reality of what I faced sank into me in ways that it never had before.

I was about to marry the man I loved. Within the hour, I would stand beside him and vow to love, honor, and trust him. And in my heart, I still wished those vows could be real.

But they couldn't.

Ronan's rejection had shocked me awake from that dream, and now, as I prepared to pay the price for all the risks I had taken, raw emotion simmered in my gut.

Agreeing to a fake marriage had been stupid, and falling in love with my fake husband-to-be made me the biggest idiot of all time.

But this situation wasn't only on me.

Over the past week, I'd searched my soul. I'd questioned and picked apart every memory of my time with Ronan. And while he'd never spoken of love, in every other way, he had behaved as if he loved me. He'd shared intimate parts of his past with me, he'd made passionate, tender love to every inch of my body, and he'd made me feel treasured in ways that no man ever had.

He'd given me hope that our story could have a happy ending.

And then he'd torn that hope away and shredded my heart.

When Cara returned, we sat down in front of the vanity, and she began applying concealer to the shadows beneath my eyes.

As she worked, I contained my emotion, until I couldn't. "I must be the dumbest woman alive," I said. "Either that, or I'm losing my mind. Part of me still can't believe all of this." I gestured at myself.

"Me. This dress. This wedding, which feels like an insane mix of fake and real."

Cara leveled me with a look. "Are you having second thoughts about going through with it?"

"No. I gave my word, and beyond that, I couldn't live with myself if I hurt Ronan that way. I can't help loving him, even if I wish I didn't. But right now, I'm angry. I'm furious with myself for getting into this mess and frustrated with Ronan's refusal to give us a chance. His whole I'm-not-capable-of-love thing is nothing but a pose, and I call bullshit on it."

"It's not a pose," Cara said as she began brushing foundation onto my face. "It may be bullshit, but it's what he truly believes."

"I get that—and I'm not asking you to take sides between me and your brother. I know how much you love him."

She sighed. "I love you both. And it kills me to see you hurting like this, but I still believe that Ronan loves you. He's crazy about you, Ava. He just needs more time to come around to admitting it."

"I wish I agreed—but I don't."

"You haven't known Ronan as long as I have," she said. "He can't be rushed, which is why I advised you to give it time before telling him how you felt."

"I couldn't go into this wedding and make vows without knowing what they meant."

"I get it," she said. "That's who you are, and in your shoes, I'd probably feel the same way. But Ronan's a man. He's different from you and me. He doesn't analyze his emotions the way we do, and he doesn't grasp his true feelings until they punch him in the gut. When that happens, as it inevitably does, he's forced to acknowledge how he really feels—which also takes time. It takes him a while to sort out his feelings, but over the next two years, he'll figure it out."

"I doubt that."

"Don't give up on him, Ava. A lot can change in two years."

"Not this," I said. "For better or worse, Ronan's made his decision. And I don't expect him to change his mind."

## 40

RONAN

Standing between an Anglican priest and my best buddy Jack, beneath the flower-bedecked ceremonial arch that had been erected on the estate's expansive lawn, I tensed as the string quartet moved into the familiar strains of Ave Maria, signaling that within minutes, I would be a married man.

A flower-lined aisle divided the hundred-plus wedding guests into two banks of smiling, expensively dressed people, who rose to their feet as first Cara, and then Ava, stepped down the aisle.

As Ava approached me, and the violin crooned Schubert's soaring melody, a chill shot down my spine. In her simple yet elegant gown, holding a bouquet of vivid flowers that complemented the ivory hue of her dress, she was the most stunning bride I'd ever seen, and for a second, my brother's words about trying to be worthy of her echoed through my mind.

She was the first woman I'd ever known who'd made me wish I was a better man. And over the past week, I'd tried to let her go, something I'd always been good at. But this time was different. Deep in my gut, I wasn't ready to let her go. Was I in withdrawal from giving up the hottest sex of my life, or was there more to it? I wasn't sure, but regardless, I felt like a grade A asshole for hurting her.

But whatever it was that I felt for Ava, part of me couldn't help but be selfishly glad that the ceremony to come was about to make her mine and buy me time to figure things out.

As I vowed to love, honor, and trust Ava, and she made the same promises to me, everything but the L-word rang true for me. I might not be a hearts-and-flowers kind of guy, but I did honor and trust her. And when I vowed to protect and shelter her for all the days of her life, I couldn't have meant those words more.

As we slipped our rings onto each other's fingers, and I claimed her lips with our first kiss as a married couple, I felt a fresh sense of resolve.

I would protect her, no matter what.

Even if in the end that meant protecting her from me.

∼

As Ava and I walked down the aisle hand in hand to the string quartet's upbeat rendition of Bruno Mars's "Marry You"—the result of a hard-won musical compromise with Veronica—our guests showered us with the rose petals that had been provided for that purpose.

"We did it," I said against Ava's ear.

"It's not over yet," she whispered.

"No, but within an hour or so, everyone will be plastered. It's all downhill from here."

When we reached the end of the aisle and began to accept the congratulations of our guests, I did my best to keep us moving toward the estate's large pergola-roofed patio, where the cocktail hour and dinner would take place. Although Ava was once again playing her role masterfully, we had a long evening ahead of us, and I thought it best to conserve our energy.

Progress was slow, but gradually we made our way through the clusters of guests now drifting toward the patio, and when we reached it, I helped Ava to her seat at the table reserved for the two of us, which was raised on a small dais so that our guests could see us.

Nearby, larger tables, draped with pristine ivory tablecloths and set with gleaming silverware and elegant floral centerpieces, ringed a central area that had been left open for after-dinner dancing. Globes of vivid flowers and ivory-hued paper lanterns hung from the pergola's wooden beams. The string quartet had been replaced with a twelve-person jazz band, which had begun playing the mixture of jazz standards and contemporary favorites that we'd requested for the evening. Most of our guests were already seated, and as I took my seat beside Ava, a smattering of applause filled the air.

As Ava and I smiled and waved, and Ava blew a kiss toward her friend Mimi, who was seated with an assortment of Hamptonites at a nearby table, the bandleader announced us as "Mr. and Mrs. Ronan Kingsley," and a dark-suited waiter rushed over with two glasses of champagne. I took them and handed one to Ava, before clinking my own against it.

"To you," I said, keeping my voice low enough that only she could hear me. "Thank you for marrying me, for being a true friend, and for always having my back."

She met my gaze and spoke quietly. "I've done my best. So have you. And the wedding's going better than expected, at least so far. Even Veronica hasn't been her usual bitchy self."

"That's thanks to a conversation Aiden had with her," I said. "I'll tell you about it later, when we're alone."

"Regardless of why, I'm grateful," Ava said.

"As am I. I'll never forget what you've done for me."

Her lips quirked in a wry half-smile, and for the first time in a week, I glimpsed a spark of humor in her eyes. "Trust me—neither will I."

## 41

### AVA

As the evening wore on, I felt increasingly claustrophobic. While Ronan couldn't have been more supportive, as we went through the rituals of a newly married couple for an increasingly raucous and inebriated audience, each moment was another stab in my battered heart.

The announcement of us as "Mr. and Mrs. Ronan Kingsley." Having our first dance—and then dancing with Ronan's father, who leered at my cleavage while holding me far too close for comfort, while Ronan whirled Veronica around the floor with a stoic expression on his face as she flashed her perfect, gleaming smile at the cream of Hamptons society. Jack's speech, in which he made the usual ribald best-man jokes about Ronan finally meeting his match.

Still, I held myself together well until the endless clinking of silverware against glasses began, demanding that we kiss—and minutes later, that we kiss again. In the past, I'd found this convention amusing, but in my current situation, it was nothing short of torture.

By the time we finished dinner, my face ached from smiling, and each kiss accelerated my internal meltdown. The single, fragile thread of hope that held me together was the knowledge that after tonight, the worst would be over.

With the wedding behind us, I'd only have to play the devoted wife now and then, at the occasional Kingsley family event or gala fundraiser. And starting tomorrow morning, I'd fix my focus on distancing myself from Ronan. Once that distance gave my heart the time and space to heal, perhaps we could manage to rebuild some degree of rapport. Not an intimate friendship, which would risk strengthening my feelings for him, but a basic level that would make it easier to share an apartment for the next two years.

I'd also refocus on my business and my passion for floral design. Burying myself in the work that I loved had saved me after my breakup with my ex-fiancé, Brian, and in time, hopefully it would save me from the heartbreak and disappointment I felt now.

Did Ronan sense my agony? If he did, he hid it flawlessly, because to my eye, he appeared relaxed, even happy. But then again, he'd gotten everything he wanted, hadn't he? I'd gone to bed with him, I'd married him, and within days, he'd have access to his $50 million trust fund.

I checked my bitter thoughts and reminded myself that while Ronan wasn't blameless in this situation, neither was I. From the day I'd met him, I'd made one mistake after another. Agreeing to a fake marriage with him. Giving in to my attraction to him. And worst of all, falling in love with him.

Tonight, the bill for those mistakes had come due.

As the clinking started up again, I resignedly leaned toward Ronan for yet another on-demand lip-lock. If I was lucky, this might be the last of the night. Although I doubted it. We weren't due to cut the cake for another half hour and would need to stay for at least another hour after that.

And as Ronan's full, sensuous lips pressed against mine for what seemed like the millionth time, my traitorous body didn't want this kiss to be our last. Couldn't want it to be our last. Despite everything that had happened between us, I loved him as much as ever—and not knowing if this was the last time he'd take me in his arms and claim my lips with his own was beyond devastating—it was tearing me apart.

This night couldn't end soon enough.

## 42

RONAN

During the week following the wedding, I was preoccupied with the legalities of gaining access to my trust, loaning ten million dollars from it to my business, and cutting Ava the $200,000 check that I'd agreed to pay her upon our marriage. It was only at the end of the week, when the dust settled, that I sensed she was avoiding me. She went to work early, she came home late, and since our wedding day, we'd barely exchanged a handful of words.

Not that I blamed her. I'd hurt her and given her every reason to back away from me. But as I awoke on Saturday morning, one week to the day after our marriage, dissatisfaction gnawed at my gut.

With the wedding behind me, and my business financially solvent, I should have been the happiest man alive—but I wasn't. Yesterday, when I'd written out the check, and Jack had slapped me on the back and congratulated me for saving Kingsley Tech, I'd felt a sense of relief but not the excitement I'd expected to feel.

And when Jack and I had gone out for a postwork drink to celebrate, although I'd done my best to join in my buddy's exuberance, I hadn't been feeling it. For such a hard-won victory, it felt surprisingly hollow to me, and given all that had happened, I attributed my lack of excitement to my guilt about hurting Ava.

Guilt. Maybe that was why I couldn't get her out of my head. It wasn't just about the sex, because although I missed that aspect of our relationship, I missed the easy rapport that we'd had together even more. I missed seeing her smile and hearing her laughter, even when it came at my expense. And if I was ever going to sort through the complicated feelings I had for her, only time together would help me figure myself out.

So, after showering, dressing, and grabbing a cup of the coffee that Ava had already made, I joined her in the living room, where she was sipping coffee and watching the morning news.

"It's been a busy week for both of us," I said.

Her gaze didn't leave the television screen. "It has."

"But now that my paperwork's in order, I'm free all weekend. Want to catch a movie this afternoon or go out for dinner tonight?"

"Can't," she said. "I have a big event proposal due Monday, so I'll be working both today and tomorrow."

"Bummer. Although it's great that your business is doing so well."

She took a sip of her coffee. "Yes—ever since you lined up that magazine article, the phone's been ringing off the hook."

"Give me a call when you head home tonight. I can throw some steaks on the grill or order takeout."

"Thanks for offering to take care of dinner," she said. "It's very thoughtful. But I'm seriously behind on this proposal. Since I need to work late, I'll probably pick up a salad or a sandwich near my office."

"Maybe tomorrow night, then."

When she looked at me, her expression was unreadable. "Sure," she said. "Maybe tomorrow."

## 43

### AVA

The first week after the wedding was hell. The second, not much better. Ronan kept pushing me to spend time with him, which I couldn't allow to happen.

Not when looking at him sent a knife through my heart, and hearing his voice made me ache for what could have been. My pain was too fresh, my emotions too raw.

But by the third week after our marriage, the Ronan-diet I'd imposed on myself began to have positive effects. While I still loved him, I felt that I was making progress on accepting the reality that we weren't right for each other. Being with him had shown me the strength of my desire for commitment, marriage, and children, and while Ronan was a good man and a fabulous lover, he wasn't ready for that kind of commitment. Perhaps he never would be.

Throwing myself into work helped, and at eight o'clock on Wednesday evening, as I sat at my desk at Oasis, catching up on my accounting for the past month, I consoled myself with the knowledge that my fledgling business was finally thriving. Maybe I wasn't over Ronan yet, but someday I would get there. For now, I just needed to maintain my current course of avoiding him as much as possible.

Which was why when my phone rang, and a glance at the screen revealed Ronan's number, I exhaled sharply, anticipating another of his invitations to have dinner or watch a movie together.

There was no point in letting it go to voicemail. If I did, he'd just call again—and again. Or he'd show up at Oasis, as he'd done last Thursday, and I'd feel obliged to suffer through an evening with him, which would only set back my recovery.

So I picked up the phone. "Hi, Ronan, what's up?"

"Bad news," he said. "I didn't want you to find out online or on TV."

He didn't sound like himself, and concern gripped me. "Are you OK? What's going on?"

"It's not me," he said. "It's my father. His helicopter went down near Long Island two hours ago."

"Oh my God, Ronan—I'm so sorry."

"I can't believe this is happening," he said, with a roughness in his voice that told me how gutted he truly was. "The Coast Guard is searching for Dad and his pilot, but it's a long shot. Even if they survived the crash, the water's too cold for anyone to stay alive for more than an hour or two."

"Are you at the apartment?"

"I am."

"I'm leaving Oasis now to catch a cab. I'll be there as soon as I can."

# 44

## RONAN

Over the days that followed, Ava was a rock. Throughout the futile search for my father's body, the eventual abandonment of that search, and the funeral, she stood by me. When I needed to talk, she listened—and when I felt lost and overwhelmed, she sat with me for hours at a time, holding my hand in silent support.

I hadn't been close to my father, but he'd been a powerful force in my life, a force that continued beyond his death in the form of the investment firm that he'd built into one of Wall Street's largest, and which was now part of his legacy to me.

Throughout my life, no matter how bad things got between me and my father, I'd always held onto a sliver of hope that someday our relationship would improve. I hadn't been aware of how much that hope meant to me, until death snatched it away.

In the days after the funeral, as I grappled with the reality of my father's will, which left me one of the wealthiest men in the world, Ava was my best advisor.

"Be true to yourself," she told me. "You don't necessarily have to do what your father would have done. Give yourself time to think each decision through, and don't let anyone rush you into anything."

Which was why, two weeks after the funeral, when I returned home from work on Friday night, I was dismayed to see a large suitcase sitting in my apartment's foyer. While my father's death made our original agreement null and void, we were still legally married, and I'd assumed that Ava would discuss any major decisions with me.

When I reached the living room, her bedroom door was open, and when I stepped into the doorway, she was leaning over a second suitcase, placing a stack of clothing inside it.

"Where are you going?" I asked.

"I've taken a vacation rental in Brooklyn for the next month," she said. "That should give me enough time to find something more permanent."

"So you're moving out."

"I only stayed this long to support you through the aftermath of your father's death," she said. "Now that our agreement is over, it's time we both got on with our lives. Which means me moving out of your apartment and the two of us getting the no-fault divorce that we both committed to. Since there's no reason to remain married for the full two years, I don't expect you to pay me any more money than you already have."

"Hold on," I said. "I don't want a divorce—at least, not yet. And I definitely don't want you to move out."

She rose to her feet, crossed her arms over her chest, and leveled me with a look. "Why not? Your business is safe, you have more money than you'll ever need, and no one can take it away from you. There's no longer any reason for us to live together, let alone stay married."

I took two steps toward her, before something in her expression stopped me and told me I needed to put everything I had on the line.

So I did. "Before our wedding, I told you I wasn't in love with you—that I wasn't capable of loving anyone in that kind of way. But now I'm not so sure."

She furrowed her brow. "What do you mean?"

"You're different from any woman I've ever known, and I can't stop thinking about you—about us. I've never been in love, so I don't know if I'm in love with you, but I'm sure about one thing—I want time to find out."

She shook her head. "If you'd said those words to me a few weeks ago, I would have gladly given you that time. But when you told me you could never return my love, it wasn't easy to choke down that bitter pill. And when I did, it forced me to face the magnitude of what I want with you and to accept that you don't want the same things."

"All I'm asking for is more time."

She sighed. "Then give me one good reason to unpack my bags."

"I thought I just did."

"Not good enough."

"I get that I hurt you," I said. "I didn't intend to, but I did. That's the real reason you don't want to be with me."

"That's not untrue, but it's a total oversimplification."

"Then complicate it for me, damn it. Tell me where you're coming from."

Her voice took on an edge of exasperation. "I love you—although right now, I really, really wish I didn't. But the fact that you drive me crazy doesn't stop me from wanting you. I want to make love to you every night and to be your wife for real. I want to be the mother of your children and spend the rest of my life with you."

"Then why are you leaving? Why—"

She cut me off. "Because loving you has made me realize what I truly want, Ronan. And I'm no longer willing to settle for anything less." She slammed her suitcase closed, turned it onto its wheels, and pulled it around me and out of the bedroom.

I followed her as she wheeled her suitcase through the living area into the foyer and attached it to the other suitcase that was already sitting there.

"Don't go," I said. "We need to figure this out together."

"There's nothing more to figure out," she said, reaching for the apartment door. "I tried to make you into someone you're not, and I'm sorry about that. But what's done is done."

And with that, she opened the door and rolled her bags through it. As the door began to swing shut behind her, I threw out my arm to hold it open, my gut twisting as I watched Ava step into the elevator.

Before the doors closed, she looked at me. "I love you, Ronan. I love you more than you know. But here's what you need to understand: I also love myself."

And with that, the doors closed, and she was gone from my life.

## 45

RONAN

Throughout the next week, I did my best to distract myself from the gaping hole that Ava's absence left in my life and absorb myself in work. On Wednesday night, I even went out to a bar with Jack, but although the women of Manhattan were as beautiful and varied as ever, I was too preoccupied with thoughts of Ava to take interest in any of them, and after two drinks, when Jack began flirting with a vivacious pixie-faced redhead, I made my excuses, called it a night, and took a cab home.

On Friday evening, when I returned to my apartment, my mail included a manila envelope containing divorce papers, which I shoved into a drawer, before calling in a pizza order and settling down in my armchair to play my favorite video game, Destiny. Eventually, I'd deal with the divorce and all that went with it, but I'd been in a lousy mood all week, and right now, I just wanted to eat pizza and shoot something.

By the time my door phone buzzed, I had shot a few hundred

cyborg warriors and eaten half of my pizza. When I hauled my ass out of the chair and answered, it was my sister, Cara.

"Come on up," I said. "If you haven't eaten already, I've got pizza."

When she arrived and stepped into the apartment, Cara surveyed the collection of discarded pizza boxes on the kitchen counter and eyed the vases of wilted flowers in the living area.

"Wow. Looks like someone's returned to bachelor living. Did your maid quit or something?"

"No, Josefina's out of town this week visiting family. Want a slice of pizza or something to drink?"

My sister shook her blond head and gestured toward the living area. "Sit down, Ronan. There's something I need to say to you."

I sat back down in my armchair, and as Cara seated herself on the couch across from me and fixed me with her bright-blue gaze, I braced myself for the lecture I sensed was coming my way.

"Earlier today, Ava told me that she'd sent you divorce papers," she said.

Annoyance simmered in my gut. "I just got them today. Did Ava send you over to make sure I sign them within twenty-four hours?"

My sister's eyes narrowed as she glared at me. "What crawled up your ass and died? Don't you dare take out your Ava-related frustrations on me. I'm not here to make you do anything—as if I even could, given how ridiculously stubborn you are. I came here to make one last attempt to save you from your own stupidity."

"If you're talking about Ava and me, it's too late," I said. "A week ago, I came home and found her packing her bags. I asked her to stay, but she turned me down and made it clear she wants nothing to do with me. She even left everything I gave her in her room—rings, dresses, shoes, the diamond earrings you helped her choose —everything."

"That makes perfect sense," Cara said. "Ava's a strong woman, and she sent you a strong message."

"By telling me she wants to be my wife and the mother of my children right before she walks out the door and sends me divorce papers?" I got up from my chair and began pacing back and forth. "What kind of fucking message is that?"

"One that any woman would understand. You're in love with her, aren't you?"

"I care about Ava. I really do. But that doesn't necessarily mean I'm in love with her."

Cara screwed up her face at me. "Are you serious? You're totally in love with her."

"How can you be so sure about that?"

"For one thing, every time you look at her, it's written all over your face," she said. "What the hell do you think being in love is, anyway?"

"I don't have a fucking definition. How would I when I've never been in love?"

"Tell me this," she said. "What do you miss most about spending time with Ava?"

"We used to laugh together a lot," I said, remembering the day I'd taken Ava to play minigolf. "I miss having coffee together every morning, and I miss our movie nights. We'd order takeout, watch a movie together, talk, make out on the couch—that kind of thing."

"How have you felt since she moved out?"

"Shitty and kind of empty inside," I admitted. "I can't get her out of my head, and I haven't been able to focus on work."

"How does Ava look in sweat pants and a T-shirt at seven a.m., with messed-up hair and no makeup?"

"What kind of a question is that?"

"Just answer me," Cara said.

"She always looks beautiful, with or without any goddamned makeup."

Cara's lips parted in a wide smile. "Congratulations, Ronan. Whether you want to admit it or not, you're in love."

I stopped pacing. Was my sister right? I had a feeling that maybe she was. Was this what love felt like? Because if it was, I'd loved Ava all along. The truth had been right in front of me, but because I'd never been in love before, I hadn't recognized my feelings for what they were. And by not recognizing the depth of my feelings for Ava, I'd completely screwed up.

"Fuck," I said, turning to face Cara. "You're right. If love means everything I've felt since Ava walked out that door, then I am in love with her. But is that enough? You know I'm not exactly ideal husband material."

"Because of Dad's history with women or your own?"

"Both."

"Don't let your fears take over," Cara said. "No one's perfect, and we all have our share of self-doubt. But right now, you have a decision to make. You can either listen to your fears and let the woman you love walk away, or you can listen to your heart, make a commitment to Ava, and resolve with everything in you to honor that commitment and make it work."

"It's not that simple," I said. "I already tried and failed to convince her to stay."

"Bullshit," Cara said. "When Ava told you she loved you and wanted a life with you, how did you respond? When she put her heart on the line, did you tell her how you feel—or did you hedge your bets and pussyfoot around?"

Understanding flooded through me. "She tried to get through to me, but I let my doubts hold me back—and now, it's too late."

"Not necessarily," Cara said. "If Ava gave you a second chance, would you take it?"

I looked my sister in the eye. "I'd seize it with both hands."

"Are you ready to do your utmost to be the man she deserves?"

"I am."

"Then I'll help you," she said, looking thoughtful. "But you're going to have to set your male ego aside if you want to have any hope of pulling this off. After all your fuck-ups, convincing Ava to give you a second chance is going to require serious groveling."

"You mean going down on my knees, like in the movies?"

"That's just the beginning."

"Sign me up," I said. "I'll do anything."

## 46

### AVA

Late Saturday afternoon, I was sitting at my worktable at Oasis, playing around with a floral centerpiece that I intended to propose to one of my new clients for her wedding reception. Vases of pink roses and carnations, larger crème roses, and delicate pale-pink limonium surrounded me, and discarded stem fragments and leaves littered my work area.

I was debating the merits of adding more limonium to the centerpiece when someone knocked on my door. "Come in," I called, reaching for a cloth to dry my hands. "It's open."

When the door opened, and Ronan appeared, I wasn't entirely surprised. He was nothing if not persistent in pursuing whatever he wanted, and when I'd moved out of our apartment, he'd made it clear that he didn't want me to leave.

In jeans and his leather bomber jacket, he was as devastatingly handsome as ever, and I steeled myself to resist an attempt to sweet-talk me into the kind of relationship he'd wanted all along. No real promises, no lasting commitments. Nothing like that. Knowing Ronan, he'd no doubt ask me again to give him time.

Which I'd already given him. Hell, I'd continued living with him for almost a full month after his father's death until I felt certain that the worst of his shock and grief had passed. I'd never loved a man as deeply as I loved him; his rejection had crushed me in ways that nothing else ever had, and right up until the moment I walked out the door of the apartment we had shared for the past few months, part of me had hoped that he'd stop me, take me in his arms, and tell me that he loved me.

But that romantic fantasy was dead. In its wake, I was determined to move on with my life, and the next step in that process was ending my marriage to him.

"Hi, Ava," he said, before closing the door and facing me. "We need to talk."

"We do," I said. "Did you get the divorce papers I sent?"

He reached inside his jacket, pulled out a folded wad of paper, and tossed it on the table in front of me. "Here's my copy. But before I sign it, there are things I need to say to you."

*Here we go.*

I brushed several stray leaves from the seat of the chair next to mine, before pushing it toward him. "Have a seat, and say what you want to say. Just don't expect it to change my mind."

He ran one hand through his hair, before he grabbed the chair, positioned it to face me, and sat down on it. "Before I begin, I need you to promise that you'll hear me out."

I furrowed my brow at him. "We're both reasonable adults."

He gave me a wry look. "Reasonable adults with hot tempers and a history of interrupting each other."

"Fine," I said. The sooner he got through whatever speech he intended to make, the sooner I could shut him down, get him to sign the divorce papers, and finish choking down today's ration of the misery I'd brought on myself by falling in love with him. "I won't interrupt you."

For a long moment, he just looked at me. "I've been an idiot, Ava.

Throughout our relationship, I've screwed up at every turn. Before I met you, I'd never fallen in love. I didn't think I was even capable of that kind of love, the kind of love you deserve. But last night, I finally understood what being in love is and realized what everything I've been feeling over the past few months truly means. I love you, Ava. I started falling in love with you soon after we moved in together, and long before our wedding day, my heart was already yours. I know I've made more than my share of mistakes, but I love you with everything in me, and if you're willing to give me a second chance, I want to spend the rest of my life with you."

For a moment, I just stared at him, speechless. Why was he telling me that he loved me? He had to know that I couldn't possibly believe him. But then the explanation dawned on me, and when it did, my anger mounted. For him, saying that he loved me was just another way of buying time—and I was having none of it.

"Where the hell is this coming from?"

"Last night, Cara helped me see the truth," he said. "I'm in love with you, just like you're in love with me."

"*Was* in love with you. In case you haven't noticed, I've moved on."

"I don't think you have."

Outraged, I leaped to my feet and glared at the man who'd first broken my heart and then trampled it to dust. If I was ever going to move on with my life and put this fake marriage behind me, I needed to put Ronan in his place once and for all. Which meant convincing him that I was over him—even if deep in my gut, I knew I wasn't.

So in an effort to protect my heart, I struck back as hard as I could. "You don't know shit about how I feel, so don't even try to go there. This is just another way of buying time for yourself, and you know something? After everything you've said and done, trying to manipulate me like this is really fucking low. Before today, I would have said that my opinion of you couldn't possibly sink lower—but congratulations. You've outdone yourself."

He stood up and reached toward me, as if to seize my shoulders, but when I stepped back from him, he dropped his arms to his sides, frustration evident on his face. "Why won't you believe me?"

My anger spilled over. "That's rich, coming from you. Do I seriously need to spell it out?"

His gaze darkened. "Throughout our relationship, I've never been anything but truthful with you. The week before our wedding, when I said I didn't love you, I was wrong—but I was telling you what I believed to be true. I've never lied to you, Ava. Not once—which is why you should believe me now."

Why was he making this so hard? I hated speaking to him so harshly, but what choice did I have, since he was refusing to get the message?

Beyond frustrated, I threw everything I had at him. "After the past two months, why the hell would I believe you? When I stood by you through our wedding, and then through your father's funeral, you never said a word—not one word—to indicate that anything had changed. And last week, when I moved out, you let me walk out that door. The only reason you're saying you love me is because you want more time, and your little talk with Cara convinced you that this is the only way to get what you want."

His eyes snapped fire. "It was no little talk, Ava. Cara helped me see that I'm in love with you, and I'm grateful to her for that."

"Whatever," I said. "I'm done arguing with you. All I want from you is your signature on the divorce papers so I can move on from this ridiculous chapter in my life."

His expression was resolute, his lips set in a firm line. "You need to accept that my feelings are real, Ava. One hundred percent real—and all mine." He held up his left hand, revealing the platinum band on his finger. "See this ring? I haven't taken it off, because I didn't want to. I still don't."

Seeing the ring on his finger nearly killed me, and my emotions threatened to overwhelm my fragile self-control. I was seconds away from melting down in front of him, which was the last thing I wanted to do. Wasn't breaking my heart enough for him? Did he have to destroy my last shred of dignity and self-respect, just to buy time? Because that's what this was—he was just trying to convince me to give him more time.

"I don't need to accept anything. You're the one who needs to improve your relationship with reality." I pointed at the divorce papers on my worktable. "See those papers? That's the reality you chose, and I refuse to argue with you any longer. If you're not willing to do the right thing and sign those papers, then you need to leave now. If you're not man enough to stand by our original agreement—which includes a no-fault divorce—then I'll just have to do this the hard way, with my lawyer's assistance."

He took a step toward me. "Look at me, Ava. Look me in the eye and tell me you don't love me. If you convince me, I swear I'll sign the divorce and leave you in peace."

I stared him down and ground out the words I needed to say, although each word was a stab in my heart. "Fine. I don't love you. Now, sign the goddamned divorce."

His eyes narrowed. "That wasn't very convincing."

I threw up my hands. "Only because you're the most stubborn, rock-headed man in existence, and no one can convince you of anything. If you're not going to sign the divorce, then get the hell out of my office."

He stepped forward, seized my shoulders, and pressed me against the wall behind me, an instant before his lips crashed down on mine. I placed my hands against his chest and shoved with all my strength, but he was immovable, and as my body betrayed me by responding to his touch, I willed myself to resist him. I had to resist him. But despite my anger, despite my resolve to push him away, something in his kiss began to penetrate the barriers I'd built to protect myself. Passionate and possessive, this kiss communicated a depth of emotion I'd never felt from him, and as his lips and tongue tasted, caressed, and ravaged mine, the walls I'd built up against him began to crack, and my certainty along with them.

Was he telling the truth? Could he really be in love with me? Because if he was, my own truth was that while I'd tried my damnedest to close my heart and push him away, I'd never truly stopped loving him. Maybe I never would.

Just before he released me from his embrace, I felt moisture against my face. And as he stepped back from me, a tear escaped his left eye and rolled down his cheek.

"Why are you crying?" I asked.

He met my gaze, his eyes dark with pain. "I guess I never thought I'd be able to kiss you again."

Was this really happening? He'd always been a rock, and I'd never seen him like this. He'd never been this vulnerable, and his face wasn't lying to me. Neither were the tears that glistened in his blue eyes.

I took a deep breath before I spoke. "Ronan, are you sure about this?"

Nothing in his expression wavered. "I've never been more sure in my life."

In that moment, my last barrier crumbled, and I finally believed him. He loved me. He was in love with me. I stepped toward him, wrapped my arms around his torso, and rested my head against his broad chest as tears welled up in my eyes, and joy streaked through my soul.

"I'm sorry," I said. "I'm sorry for everything I just said to you. I thought you were just trying to buy time, but now I see that you aren't."

"You're not to blame," he said. "This is on me."

"I can't believe that we're here—but I'm so happy that we are."

For a long time, we just held each other, absorbing the wonder of the moment. When we finally released each other, Ronan cleared his throat, before dropping to one knee in front of me.

"This time around, I'm doing it right," he said.

For the second time today, he'd surprised me, and my lips curved in a smile. "I never realized you were superstitious."

"When it comes to you, I'm not prepared to push my luck any further than I already have." He reached into his jacket pocket and pulled out two familiar rings—my engagement ring and my wedding band—before looking up at me. "Stay married to me, Ava. Be my wife and the mother of my children. I don't deserve you, and no doubt I never will, but if you stay married to me, I swear to spend the rest of my life loving you and doing my best to be worthy of you."

Smiling through my tears, I held out my left hand to him. "Yes. A million times yes. I love you, and there's nothing I've ever wanted more."

Joy spread across his upturned face as he took my hand, lifted it to his lips, and kissed it, before slipping the two rings onto my finger and running his thumb over their glittering stones. I put my other hand over his, intending to tug him to his feet and seal our renewed marriage with a kiss.

"Take me home, Ronan," I said. "Let's start our new life together."

"I will," he said. "But before we go home, there's one more thing I need to do."

"What's that?"

He gazed into my eyes. "When we said our wedding vows, I know you meant yours, but I was confused about parts of mine—which is why I want to say them to you again now."

When he said that, I couldn't help tearing up again as he began the simple but profound vows we had chosen for our wedding ceremony.

"I, Ronan, pledge myself to you, Ava. I promise to love, honor, and trust you and to protect you and shelter you. I promise to be a loving husband to you and a devoted father to our children. I promise to stand by you and support you through every challenge we face together and to be your true, loyal partner, lover, and friend for all the days of our lives."

When he had finished, he got to his feet and pulled me into a searing kiss, a kiss like no other we'd ever shared. Tender and possessive, this kiss spoke of love, with a deep undercurrent of the promises just made, and as he held me in his arms and kissed me with everything in him, I knew beyond a shadow of a doubt that we belonged together. He might be the most stubborn man on earth, and he had a temper that rivaled my own, but he was my stubborn, hot-tempered man—and today, he'd made my dreams come true.

"Let's make tonight our true wedding night," he said when we came up for air. "With time and space for us to have our way with each other, like a couple of newlyweds should."

I leaned back and cupped his handsome face in my hands. "You know something? That's a genius idea."

His lips quirked, before parting in a smile. "There's a first time for everything." Without releasing me, he reached out with one hand, grabbed the divorce papers from my worktable and crumpled them into a ball. "But before we head home, is there a metal trashcan or sink around here? I'd like to burn these fucking papers."

He couldn't have suggested a more meaningful gesture to mark our new beginning.

"Let's use the utility sink," I said, reaching for his hand. "We'll burn them together."

# AFTERWORD

Thank you for reading *Heir of the Hamptons*! Cara's story will continue in *Park Avenue Player*, which will be released in early 2018.

I know that your time is valuable and sincerely thank you for finishing this book! If you would take a moment to return to where you purchased the book and leave a review it would be much appreciated.

Reviews provide valuable feedback to me as a writer, and help fellow readers decide if they might enjoy this book.

This page on my website contains a list of my books and links to all retailers who carry them, to save you from needing to search for the book's page in order to leave your review.

Thank you again, and be sure to check out my other books here!


**Get the latest on new and upcoming releases!**

Find me on Facebook at https://www.facebook.com/ErikaRhys.Author

I'm on Facebook often and enjoy chatting with my readers.

Join my mailing list at http://erikarhys.com/subscribe/. List members receive about one email a month featuring free ARC, giveaway, and book release announcements.

Your email will NOT be shared with anyone else, and you can unsubscribe from the list at any time—although I hope you'll choose to stay!

Printed in Great Britain
by Amazon